There she stood.

Staring at him from the other side of the long, freshly oiled wooden bar. She was covered in ivory satin, blond hair slipping out from a silken braid that trailed down one shoulder, cheeks taut and scuffed with dirt, with a piercing look of determination in those big brown eyes.

Harrison inhaled deeply, stunned by her sudden presence. Even more so at her appearance. He wasn't normally speechless, but then he'd never been surprised in this town by a pretty woman he didn't know or recognize. He bristled as he contemplated any reason why she might be here, a runaway bride with one sleeve torn. Dirty, frightened and alone.

* * *

Alaska Bride on the Run
Harlequin® Historical #999—July 2010

Praise for Kate Bridges

ALASKAN RENEGADE
Nominated for Best Western of the Year by
Love Western Romances
"The wild north heats up whenever Bridges brings
her alpha heroes and strong-willed heroines together in a
battle-of-wills romance. There's always enough adventure,
passion and atmosphere to entertain every Western reader."
—*RT Book Reviews*

WANTED IN ALASKA
"Bridges brings strong, admirable heroes and
independent-minded women to life. There's nothing better
in these cold locales than her stories laced with humor,
passion and danger."
—*RT Book Reviews*

KLONDIKE FEVER
"Humor, sensuality and high adventure."
—*RT Book Reviews*

KLONDIKE WEDDING
"Likable characters and an engaging storyline that keeps
the reader entranced the whole way through."
—*Romance Junkies*

KLONDIKE DOCTOR
CataRomance Reviewers' Choice Award Winner
for Best Historical
"Her heroes are the strong silent type, and it's simply
delightful to watch them fall in love with her headstrong
heroines. Not only is the romance wonderful,
the unique backdrop adds another fascinating
dimension to a terrific story."
—*RT Book Reviews*

THE COMMANDER
Barclay Gold Award Winner for Best Historical
"An emotionally intense, wonderfully satisfying tale
of love and redemption."
—*Booklist*

Recycling programs
for this product may
not exist in your area.

ISBN-13: 978-0-373-29599-9

ALASKA BRIDE ON THE RUN

www.eHarlequin.com

Printed in U.S.A.

KATE BRIDGES

Alaska Bride on the Run

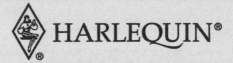

HARLEQUIN®

TORONTO • NEW YORK • LONDON
AMSTERDAM • PARIS • SYDNEY • HAMBURG
STOCKHOLM • ATHENS • TOKYO • MILAN • MADRID
PRAGUE • WARSAW • BUDAPEST • AUCKLAND

This book is dedicated with much gratitude and best wishes to all my readers. It's a pleasure hearing from you, and getting to know where some of you have traveled in Alaska and the Yukon.

Chapter One

District of Alaska, August 1899

When Harrison Rowlan placed the sign in the window of his new tavern, calling for a bartender, he didn't expect a woman in a torn wedding gown to apply.

Harrison was stacking kegs of ale against the back wall when she first entered his empty bar. Warm morning sunshine streamed in from the windows. Humming to himself, he slid the heavy slosh of liquid off his shoulder and inhaled the earthy scent of the wood. His tavern and adjoining livery stables here in the town of Eagle's Cliff weren't officially open yet. He still had two days to go.

However, he was pleased to be making steady headway in obtaining supplies from the much larger Skagway harbor, twenty miles south, and had already hired six of the seven employees he needed, including extra security for his stables. With the recent news of the gang of horse thieves pillaging the coast and valleys, armed guards were an unexpected necessity.

Harrison preferred to own a tavern rather than a rowdy saloon. His tavern would be a neighborhood place for local patrons to drop by not only for a pint of brew and a solid meal, but also where a person might meet up with a friend, exchange dated newspapers from home, pick up mail, or listen to the only entertainment available in town.

Footsteps sounded behind him. He turned around too fast and the rib muscles that were still healing from the knife wound he'd received earlier this summer twisted. He winced with the annoyance.

There she stood.

Staring at him from the other side of the long, freshly oiled wooden bar. She was covered in ivory satin, blond hair slipping out from a silken braid that trailed down one shoulder, cheeks taut and scuffed with dirt, with a piercing look of determination in those big brown eyes.

He inhaled deeply, stunned by her sudden presence. Even more so at her appearance. He wasn't normally speechless, but then he'd never been surprised in this town by a pretty woman he didn't know or recognize. He bristled as he contemplated any reason why she might be here, a runaway bride with one sleeve torn. Dirty, frightened and alone.

He couldn't think of one.

His right hand instinctively dropped to the gun strapped to his thigh. Ready for anything. Wasn't he always? Not that he feared this unarmed slender woman, a head shorter than himself and half the width of his shoulders, but rather the trouble she might be bringing with her. He'd had enough of that, running from the law the past two years before he'd finally cleared his name of the crimes he'd been mistakenly and maliciously accused of. His face had been plastered on Wanted posters all over the district.

"This sign," she said, holding the cardboard that he'd stuck into the front window ten days ago when he'd bought the place, "is why I'm here."

He looked down at the words she clutched between grimy fingers—Bartender Wanted.

He assessed the situation with a quick look to the front windows and doors. The freshly painted outdoor sign hanging from the covered boardwalk tilted in the wind, declaring Eagle's Cliff Tavern and Inn. There was no one out there. No one following her. At least, not right now. Judging by the streaks of dirt across her gown, and her ruffled hair, she'd been on the road for a couple of days.

"Miss? Or is it missus? You in some sort of trouble?"

"It's miss…and…yes, I am." Her voice was soft and rich, and he tried to stop himself from enjoying the view. "I'd be mighty grateful if—" she glanced over her shoulder "—if you could take me to…to your kitchen and we might have a talk."

It was one of those situations—and he'd known plenty in the past couple of years from being on the run himself—where he had to make a quick decision.

Did he help this stranger or not?

Should he get involved, or worry about his own hide and the new life he was attempting to make for himself?

Looking down into her face, the way the angle of light hit her soft jawline and bounced over the curve of her lips, he told himself her problems were not his.

Even if she looked more like an angel than a troublemaker. He damn well knew better.

But blazes, his chest tightened and his pulse rippled inside his skin at seeing the lovely lady. The least he could do would be to offer shelter for a moment, explain the route to the Skagway deputy marshal, who was the nearest lawman, twenty miles south—a full day's ride since the coastline was so treacherous—and point her to the women's store on the boardwalk, where she could buy proper clothing.

He stepped out from the bar, a head taller than her, and waved his hand toward the back hall. "This way."

He led her through the doorway. His leather vest squeaked over the white cloth of his shirt as he twisted his shoulders. Denim jeans fit snugly on his thighs.

When they reached the huge kitchen with its two walk-in fireplaces, the simmering pots of stew and the shelves of dishes, he turned, nearly bumping into her. He quickly stepped away, giving her distance.

"I need a job," she panted.

First thing's first. Her comfort. He slid the cardboard sign from her slender fingers, placed it on the counter and offered her a stool.

She hesitated, then looked about the room. He watched her gaze skim the hanging herbs, the dry sink in the corner, which was no more than a cabinet with buckets for washing dishes, various shelves and sundries. Her eyes flickered on the closed back door. A route of escape, she was no doubt thinking. Slowly, she sank onto the stool. Ivory satin billowed about her feet.

"Nice train."

Her eyes widened, then a smile darted across her lips. Of course, she must be aware of her unusual choice of clothing. He was trying to set her at ease, and the comment worked.

His gaze lowered to her wedding gown. The top part, the part with the neckline, plunged daringly to her cleavage. A golden necklace anchored itself between her breasts, beyond his vision. He rubbed his neck to distract himself.

The gown seemed a bit too large for her, but who was he to criticize fashion? Besides, here in Alaska, where everything had to be shipped in due to the shortage of supplies, folks took and used what they could.

"Not the marrying kind?"

She straightened her spine. Her neckline gaped in response, revealing the top of a black lace corset. His pulse leaped involuntarily. He ordered his eyes to remain focused on her face.

"Not the anything kind. I'm my own person."

"How does *he* feel about that?"

"Not taking it well."

"Is he chasing you?"

She inhaled a rush of air. "I think he and his men assume I ran to the docks. In Skagway. That I left for the lower States on the first ship out."

His men? What odd words. *Not his friends? Not his groomsmen?*

"Why would they think that?"

"Because I left them false clues. Told them I was running home."

She looked toward the fires. Both stone fireplaces sputtered and popped with heat as cauldrons boiled within them. Pots also simmered on the stoves. The cooks had been in earlier and had started on the stews, then they'd left for the market.

Harrison kept the conversation on topic. "Where's home?"

She didn't answer right away. She breathed in the aromas of the kitchen. The tightness in her cheeks relaxed. Her firm bottom lip softened. "This place."

"Nooo," he said, planting his palm in the air. "Let's just hold on here a minute." He leaned against the counter that jutted from the side wall, surrounded by stacks of dishes and glassware. His massive frame barely squeezed in. He crossed his cowboy boots and remained calm. No matter how attractive she was, it would be a bad business decision on his part to let her stay. Hell, it would also be a bad personal decision. "I don't have a job for you."

Her eyes flashed. "I'd make a fabulous bartender."

"The position's open for a man."

"I could do it."

He crossed his arms. "That might be. But the position's open for a man."

Her slender throat bobbed, caught in some emotion he didn't wish to analyze. She looked down to her lap, where she was knotting her fingers together.

He hadn't asked for her name yet. On purpose. The less he knew, the less likely he'd be suckered in by a woman.

"Why?" Her voice echoed softly off the uprooted herbs hanging from the ceiling. "Why's it open only to a man? In Skagway, a woman runs one of the casinos. Another *owns* a tavern. Maybe in the lower States, the position of bartender might be unusual. But not in Alaska. Women do all kinds of things here."

She was right. Women owned jewelry shops, worked as apothecaries, printers, barbers, and he even knew of a female blacksmith. But it didn't mean he was looking for a woman.

Women were scarce in Alaska, he guessed maybe only ten to fifteen percent of the population. The stamina it took to cross the ocean, then the mountains to the Klondike by foot if they were in search of gold, meant only the toughest and most independent arrived.

He took out a bowl from underneath the counter, walked to the pot of stew and ladled out a steaming heap of beef and potatoes. Moving closer, he placed the hearty meal in front of her, along with warm biscuits.

Her eyes misted in gratitude. She picked up the spoon. "Thank you."

It wasn't often he got a chance to watch a beautiful woman eat. She cracked the biscuit and dipped the spoon into the stew with grace, head held high, despite the mussed-up hair and the smudge of dirt across her chin.

Whoever had let her go would want her back. He would.

"Did you notice, on your escape between Skagway and here," he said, hauling fresh logs to the fireplace to give her privacy to eat, "that Alaska is filled with men? When this place opens, it'll be packed with fishermen, explorers, lumberjacks. Gold miners who cuss so loud and hard your eardrums rattle. A rough place. No place for a woman."

"Well, I did grow up with eight boys on a ranch."

Hmm. Nice try to get him to care. He refused to dig deeper into her personal life.

"Aren't any of your employees ladies?"

He poked at the red embers. "The cook is. But I hired her as a team with her husband. And two of the barmaids who double as singers and piano players. But they're both used to working around men. The bartender's got to be a man. Able to stop fights. Able to keep the tabs straight. Knows what a working man likes to drink."

"Mead. Bourbon. Scotch. How about those kegs of beer and ale you were unloading in the bar? Stout, bitters, milds, porters. You name it, I've poured it."

"You've worked in a bar before?"

The sparkle in her brown eyes dampened. "Not exactly. But I grew up with eight male cousins and one demanding uncle. They're the main reason, I suppose, that I got stuck in this mess." She looked down at her gown. "Everyone always telling me how to run my life. I served them a lot of meals and a lot of drinks."

"The answer's no."

She dabbed her lips on a napkin. Then stood up, tidied her dishes and brought them to the dry sink by the window. When she turned around again, her gaze shifted to a ball of twine and a pair of scissors.

She lunged for the weapon.

He reached for his gun, but there was no need to panic.

In a combination of disbelief and amusement, he watched her use the scissors to hack off her torn sleeve. Then she went for the other one to match. Next, she attacked her train. In a maneuver he found mesmerizing, she bent over and slit her dress just above the floor, wiggling till she got it fairly even, exposing the tips of shiny black boots, buckled up real high around her ankles. The kind of boots he'd always found seductive.

She returned the scissors and threw the scraps of fabric into the crackling fire. Her eyes spotted a pile of empty burlap sacks in the corner, ones the cooks had emptied of various vegetables bought off the incoming ships. She searched for the cleanest one and then draped it over her shoulders as a makeshift shawl.

Her eyes sought his for permission.

He shrugged. "You can have it."

Mighty resourceful of her. And what a change. The burlap shawl covered much of her upper body, and cut the ivory color in half so it wouldn't be so glaring and noticeable from a distance. Now sleeveless, the gown looked more like a pretty summer dress.

"I'll go." She moved toward the door. "Quietly. I'll slip out this back way and I won't bother you another minute. But first, I'd appreciate an honest answer to one question."

He quirked an eyebrow and strode to the door to open it, eager for her to leave. He didn't like the uncomfortable squeeze in his chest that she'd produced since arriving. Besides, his work was piling up and by the time he walked her to the shops, he'd lose another thirty minutes.

"One question usually leads to another," he told her firmly. "And I've got work to finish in the front room."

She tried a different tactic. "My name—"

He stopped her with a motion of his hand. "No need for names, either. I'll walk you to the hotel down the road. You can write your pretty little name in the registry book. The hotel I've got in mind is fairly safe. The proprietor's an old widow, and she knows how to use a shotgun."

He had a few spare rooms upstairs, but he planned on renting them out.

"Just one question? Please."

He set his jaw straight, ignoring her plea, determined not to argue or extend this any longer than necessary. Leaning past her shoulder, he yanked open the back door. A stream of sunshine poured in around the draped burlap that covered her shoulders. In an odd way, the brown sack accented the warmth of her brown eyes and golden hair.

He pointed past the garden. "There's a women's store two blocks down. I'll walk you there. We don't have any lawmen in town, but I'll help you contact the deputy marshal's office in Skagway. That's your best bet to get your would-be groom off your back. Let's go."

She didn't move. She jutted her chin in refusal. An

odd stance, considering she was in such desperate circumstance and he was the only one around helping her.

She had a fiery spirit, which was the other likely reason, besides her cousins and uncle, for what had gotten her into this sticky situation.

Her lashes flickered. "You want to fill your tavern when it opens, don't you?"

"Come on, lady, I've got work to do. I'll make sure you're safe. I'll even pay the bill for the hotel. I'll give you a few bucks to get you back to Skagway. Whatever you need. Now, after you." He nodded to the outdoors, indicating she step out first.

Still, she wasn't budging.

And despite his refusal to hear her one and only question, she gave it to him anyway. "You're starting a new business. You want it to be successful." Sunlight caught the side of her downy cheek. "You said your patrons will be mostly men. Don't you think those men would prefer an interesting new woman pouring their drinks, rather than some bearded old guy everyone in town already knows?"

Willa knew by the look in his eyes that she'd hit a soft spot with her question. Of course he'd be affected by talk of increased sales. What owner wouldn't be?

Especially this man. Peering up at him as his mouth twisted and his firm, tanned cheeks pulled back, Willa waited as he grappled for an answer. He wanted his business to flourish. It hadn't taken her long to size him up when she'd walked in.

The newly painted sign hanging off the front awning gave him away. It was full of pride, the glossy green paint and ornate wrought-iron details, the handsome depiction of two men bowing to each other. Then there was the sparkling bartop that glistened with polish. The bar was made of mahogany—unusual for this part of the world—and no doubt imported. And the neatly stacked kegs of spirits. Even the kitchen was bursting with fresh foods and brand-new drinking glasses.

Then there was the man himself, dressed in a white shirt and brown leather vest that accentuated his black hair and dark eyes. He stood toned and muscled. With his freshly scraped jaw, he still had a hint of shaving cream on his skin. Everything about his movements told her he was trying to nudge her out the door so he could get back to his first love—his tavern.

"Who sent you here?"

Her face skewered. How could he possibly know someone had advised her? But she trembled beneath the dangerous stare and decided she needed to tell him straight. "Stew MacGuinness."

"Ah. One of the dozens of men who runs a boat from Skagway, up the coast and back."

"Yes, sir. He put in a good word for you. Told me you might need an extra hand."

He paused and watched her. She shuffled to her other foot, so weary from her night's travel. Heat crawled up her cheeks at his perusal, at her proximity to yet another stranger. "He…is a man to be trusted, is he not? He swore he wouldn't tell a soul he took me."

"Yeah, he's trustworthy. Especially since you likely didn't give him your real name."

The hot flame of embarrassment flicked at her throat. This man would not be easily fooled.

"What name did you give him?"

"Willa Banks."

He studied her hard and she tried not to flinch.

Part of her name was true. Her real name was Mary Somerset. Willa was her middle name and she'd always preferred to use it over Mary. Her uncle had first teased her with it when she was a tyke who'd defended her toys and space from her older cousins, whenever they'd ganged up on her. Willa, he'd told her, meant fierce defender.

It seemed that for her whole life, she'd been trying to live up to the name. What was she here on earth to defend?

Willa Banks had been her secret play name as a child with her best friend, Madeleine, when they'd dressed up and pretended to be lady pirates on the high seas. Madeleine had moved away a year after Willa's mother had died, but Willa had never forgotten the secret surname. Back in Skagway, her wretched would-be groom, Keenan Crawford, had never heard of Willa anyone. When she'd arrived in Alaska, she'd used the name on her papers, Mary Somerset.

That's who he was looking for now. *If* he was still looking.

Perhaps Willa Banks would be a rebirth. A reconnection with her lost childhood friend, and maybe to her vanished mother.

The tavern owner in front of her stepped through the back door into the gardens. She followed, inhaling the scents of plush turned soil, ripe herbs and vegetables. Benches lined the property. They were enclosed by buildings on both sides.

"If you stay," he said, "I don't wish to know anything personal about you."

A shiver of delight raced through her. She tugged on the burlap. Bees darted around them, through the smattering of willow trees and pines. "You mean I'm hired?"

Her uncle in Montana would be outraged at her working as a bartender, but he had outdated standards. Hers were much more modern, in the vein of other Alaskan women. She'd be protected here, surrounded by the men of Eagle's Cliff. There were no telegraph lines to Skagway, no easy communication between the towns, and no reason for anyone to come looking for her here.

"You've got a few more questions to answer." He rubbed the dark wave of hair above his ear. "Why me?"

"Mr. MacGuinness told me about your problems with the law. He—he showed me an old Wanted poster with your face on it. Explained how it had been a mistake and your name was now clear."

"And you figured that would soften me to *your* plight?"

"Yes, Mr. Rowlan."

The man frowned at the use of his name. "And why a bartender?"

"I need to make some money to get where I'm going. Can't save much on a woman's salary. Not at a dress shop. Not as a cashier. Or laundress. Bartending will earn me tips on top of my wages. I'll make more than I ever could working in a woman's job, and you'll make more hiring me."

"I can't pay you like a man."

"Why not?"

"You're a woman. It's just not done. Half salary is appropriate."

"Which is?"

"Fifty cents a night. But you get to keep all your tips."

"Fifty cents," she negotiated boldly, "plus one percent of the increased sales I'll be bringing in."

"One percent? You're jumping the gun. How do you know sales would increase since I haven't opened yet?"

She faltered. "Mr.—Mr. MacGuinness coached me a little. On what to ask for."

"Did he now?" His fierce look made her back down.

"All right, I'll take the full dollar a night. Plus all my own tips."

"Lady, you're tougher than you look."

"That's the kind of person you want working behind your bar, isn't it? Someone who can hold their own with a man?"

He paced the plot of vegetables, rubbing his neck. His shoulders cast long shadows on the stone path. Lord, he was bigger and more muscled than any of her eight cousins, and they were all physically fit from working on the ranch.

When he turned around, his dark intensity caused her stomach to flutter.

"One week. Trial period. If you don't work out, I'm free to let you go."

She swallowed, scared to believe it. Scared not to. "All right." Moving closer, she held out a tentative hand and they shook.

His grip was firm, businesslike and manly.

"One week," she agreed.

He spun on his big cowboy boots, leaning into the gentle wind, motioning her toward the boardwalk and shops visible beyond the stretch of his shoulders.

But she didn't wish to go to the other hotel. Squinting in the sun, she gazed up at the second story of his tavern. The muscles in her stomach turned and twisted again. How would she tackle her next question?

Chapter Two

❦❧❦

"I know what you're thinking and I don't much like it." Harrison waited for Willa to follow him to the shops, but he stood alone in the bright sunshine while she studied his tavern. The scent of scrub pines reached his nostrils.

"What do you mean?" Willa nervously wrapped her fingers around her bare throat, as if challenging his assumption. Her fine gold necklace glistened off her skin, with the medallion reaching somewhere between her breasts.

"The rooms I have upstairs are for rent. To strangers."

"Well, I am a stranger. I was hoping…" She peered up at the second story, her blond braid twisting like a skein of silk around her shoulders. "Hoping there might be something small tucked into a back corner? Something that's not prime renting space? You could take it out of my salary."

"It'd be a little too close for comfort. Arm's distance. I prefer that with all of my employees."

"But…I'd feel much safer staying under your roof. I don't know anyone else in Eagle's Cliff. And if I'm bartending, I'll be walking home in the middle of the night. You know the safety concerns that might cause."

He crossed his arms. He would not be railroaded into anything…but her safety *was* an issue. If she were living right above the bar, then he wouldn't have to walk her home in the wee hours of the morning.

Less concern and less time wasted for him.

"You'd feel safer under my roof? Then someone *is* coming after you. Your groom."

"I already said…I don't think so. He thinks I'm headed back to Montana."

"Why didn't you just tell him you don't want to marry him?"

Fear flickered in her eyes. "Kind of hard to do with a gun glued to my head."

Harrison winced. He'd met many bullies like that one, shoving their way to the gold fields, snatching whatever they pleased. Assaulting women.

"What's his name?"

Her mouth dropped open in surprise.

"I'll need to know. To protect you. And to protect myself."

"Surely, there's no need—"

"If you don't trust me, then you should send word to the deputy marshal in Skagway that you're in trouble."

"That'll only alert *him* that I'm here!"

Terror grooved lines into her forehead. Circles deepened beneath her eyes. There was no sense upsetting her further. But Harrison *would* get the name out of her when she calmed down. "Well, there are other women here, as you said. The cook. Plus a housekeeper that comes in to do the rooms. They're all respectable."

Except that Willa was the most striking. The other two were matronly types. Not as curvy or spellbinding.

However, talking to Willa—or whoever she was—for just one minute would give anyone the impression that she was decent. Maybe she'd add sophistication to the place. Some class and charm. That's what he was selling, wasn't he? A neighborhood place where folks could leave their worries at home and come here for a bite to eat during the day, and a stiff drink in the evenings?

He should point out another fact. "I *also* live above the bar."

Her cheeks flushed at the disclosure. She glanced away from his face to the vegetables. "It's not as if the two of us would be living alone." She nudged the dirt with her boot. "There's a shortage of roadside inns and lodges in Alaska. I'm sure your rooms will have no trouble filling."

"True enough. Half of them are already reserved for opening night."

"If you give me a room now, I'd be pleased to go on to the shops myself and buy some clothes. Save you some time."

But he noticed she wasn't carrying a satchel or purse.

"You've got money?"

"A bit." She lowered her lashes.

He didn't want to know where she was hiding it. He cleared his throat, and for the second time in the past hour, relented to the runaway bride.

He took a step forward, towering above her shoulders. "Follow me. There's a room in the upper corner you can have." When he brushed past her, her necklace flashed in the sunlight, reminding him again of the warm place it was nestled in. He swallowed hard, forcing himself to look straight ahead as he took her through the kitchen, the bar and up the newly varnished staircase.

Eyes off the hired help, he warned himself. She was a woman in deep trouble with matrimony problems, and he would stay as far away as possible.

The man carried a gun and seemed to notice every detail around him. That's why, Willa told herself, moving in under his roof made the most sense. She wasn't about to leave Alaska and give up on her dreams because of one twisted man who'd tried to force her into marriage. She'd blend in here with the other women of Eagle's Cliff. She had to flee somewhere for protection until Keenan Crawford's appetite for her subsided, so why not here?

She followed Harrison up the stairs, his wide shoulders taking up a good span, his big cowboy boots barely fitting on each tread. They crossed the carpeted hall, dipped past the railing and balcony that overlooked the bar below, and headed straight back into the corner.

He got to the last door on the south side, turned the knob and pushed it open, allowing her to enter first.

It smelled clean.

It wasn't big, but sunshine bathed the room and when she stepped to the window, she delighted in the view of the ocean. Deep blues and greens swirled along the rocky coastline. Mountains on her right rose to the top of the clouds, and if she stretched on tiptoe, she could see the curved inlet that formed the harbor.

"Smallest one I've got. I'm staying on the other side of the hall, on the far end. You'll have privacy here."

The embarrassing tinge of heat rippled up her neck. Why must her body give away her feelings? Why couldn't she just look up into the handsome face and coolly say thank-you?

"Thank you."

"There's a ladies' room across the hall. Men's

room is on the other end, so you won't be disturbed. Bathing takes place on the main floor in a steam room off the kitchen."

"Sounds convenient. The bathing room I mean."

"You don't have much to wear—"

"I've got enough money for clothing."

His gaze strayed down her bodice.

She felt warm again. "I would appreciate directions to the shop you mentioned." She noted the basin and towel on the nightstand. "I'll go after I tidy up."

Tension left his face. Perhaps because he no longer had to use any more of his precious time with her, and could get back to his chores. "Straight out the back door. Turn right and follow the boardwalk for two blocks. It's called Lily's Laces. Best prices and best selection in town. So their sign says."

Her burlap shawl slid down her shoulders. "Thank you, Mr. Rowlan."

"Harrison."

"Harrison it is." She paused. "You won't tell anyone here, will you?" Her mouth quivered. "About my problems?"

"No," he assured her. "Not until you're ready. And I should've asked earlier. Are you hurt anywhere?" His eyes strayed down her body again and she wished the wedding gown thrust upon her weren't so low-cut.

His eyes bounced back quickly from her neckline. He cleared his throat and took a step back against the doorway.

"Nothing serious. My shins are a bit bruised from crawling out of the minister's office. And my knee twisted slightly when I jumped onto the horse for the getaway, but…I'll be fine after a light rest."

He was smiling.

She was taken aback by the warmth in his expression and the humor that came naturally to him. Her story *did* seem rather ridiculous. However, she warned herself not to trust him, or any person. She'd put her trust into strangers in Skagway, and look where that had gotten her. And sadly, at home, trusting her uncle and cousins hadn't worked in her favor, either. At least Harrison had come highly recommended, and his clearance from being wanted by the law gave her some relief.

"Enjoy your rest."

And he was gone.

She plopped onto the bed. It was pleasantly firm, not at all lumpy as she'd expected. Must be a new mattress. Where was he getting the funds to invest in this place?

It didn't matter. He seemed as keen to make the business a success as she was to prove her worth.

As hard as she'd worked in Montana with her uncle and cousins, no one had ever noticed her value. Only what it might do for them—the backbreaking work she'd done in the stables, the hours and hours of sewing and mending for nine men. She hadn't been allowed to leave or marry before each of her cousins had, so that she'd be available to look after them at home. A built-in housekeeper, cook and, perhaps when children came to her cousins, also a built-in nanny. It would have been a never-ending cycle of hard work.

What was wrong with wanting a life of her own? Her opportunity had come. She'd left her old life behind and still had no regrets.

She stared up at the rafters.

"Willa." She said the name aloud, taking pleasure in how it rolled off her tongue. "Willa Banks." The first name sounded carefree; the surname sturdy and reasonable. Just as she hoped to be.

So much more carefree than the past ten years of her life. Although she'd loved every acre of the ranch from corner to corner, and worked as long and hard as any of them, she was never promised a piece of it.

"It'll go to my eldest son," her uncle had declared one evening as she was clearing the dinner plates.

She was only ten at the time—and dumb—for she'd thought she belonged in that family. *"Can I have a corner of it by the river, sir? Just a little piece? Something to set me up so when it comes time to brand my own cattle—"*

She had gotten only that far when her cousins had burst out laughing.

"You'll have to wed your way into some prop-

erty," they'd told her as she'd scraped their plates. *"You can't expect our pa just to give you some."*

But there was so much of it. In her ten-year-old eyes, there was enough for everyone. Her parents didn't have a thing of their own to pass down to her, they'd died so young.

Tired of being ignored, she saw no way out. Until one morning this spring, she'd seen the advertisement in the local paper on the bustling business in Skagway, and its servicing the gold miners of the Klondike. When she'd read about some women who'd also found their fortune here, she'd known in that instant, like a clap of thunder, that Alaska was in her destiny.

She'd left Montana with no more than a note. If she'd confided in any of them, they would've stopped her, like they had the time she'd wanted to enter the rodeo and they'd locked her in her room for a week till it had passed. Her bedroom walls had heard more crying and cusswords than she'd ever admit to anyone.

The voyage on the ship hadn't been easy, either. And when she'd gotten to Skagway, she'd made the mistake of befriending one of the local businessmen.

Keenan Crawford. The town butcher.

His hands were as raw and thick as the meat he hammered, but it was his charming way of serving her that drew her into his shop twice a week. He'd poured on the compliments, silly ones she wasn't accustomed to, too naive to realize he had ulterior motives.

A bird twittered from behind the window curtain of her room at the inn. With a sigh, she stood up, walked to the basin, poured some water and scrubbed her face.

The round mirror tacked to the wall reflected how difficult the past forty-eight hours had been. Bluish circles rimmed her eyes. Dirt streaked her chin.

One morning, when she'd unexpectedly walked into the back room of the butcher shop, she'd overheard Crawford talking with his crude friends. The first part of the conversation had seemed normal. Something about arranging times to meet the following night, about delivery of cattle and market prices of beef. Then when he noticed her, he'd leered at her breasts and snickered with his insinuating remarks. *"Fine ribs. Gorgeous cut of leg."*

She'd only come in for some lean meats, but knew she'd never be back to his shop again. By the time she was paying at the till, she'd had enough of his remarks. He'd licked his lips at her rear end and muttered, *"Nice rump roast."* His friends had snickered.

Then she replied, *"Go stuff your sausage somewhere else."*

She'd been hoping for a bit of humor, or something, but there'd only been dead silence. He didn't smack her in front of his friends. In fact, he'd never smacked her in the weeks she'd known him. But she could see in his gleaming little eyes and the way his fist came up instinctively that he would beat her with all his power, one day, if she let him.

When she'd told her fears to her female acquaintances at the boarding house, they'd told her she was crazy. And when Crawford had come to the parlor that evening and had asked for her hand in marriage, those acquaintances told her how much she had to gain by marrying one of Skagway's most successful businessmen.

"No," she'd told him, tugging him up off the floor as he'd bent on one knee. *"No thank you, Mr. Crawford. I'm not the right bride for you."*

His broad head had turned beet-red and he hadn't said another word.

Not until he'd shown up in the middle of the night with one too-large wedding gown, and the cold barrel of a six-shooter pressed to her temple.

Worst of all... She cringed at the memory. Worst of all, he'd clawed her nightgown up to her waist, revealing the shame of her nakedness, and put his hand down there.

His fingers had been as cold and rough as twisted metal. *"You know what I'd like to do to you?"*

"Please," she'd begged, wishing she could crawl beneath the covers and never come up for air.

His collar had smelled like sour milk. *"You'll be my wife."* His voice was a snarl, not at all loving and kind, the way a future husband's voice should be.

Somehow, she'd pulled together a breath of courage to divert him. *"Mr. Crawford...Keenan...I would truly wish to wait for this...wonderful moment till after our wedding vows are said."*

He'd looked at her through calculating eyes. *"What's that?"*

"If we wait, it'll be more special. I could—" she swallowed hard to hide her revulsion. *"I could prepare and wear something lacy and lovely for you."*

He'd stopped what he was doing and let out a low lecherous laugh.

He'd almost raped her. She squeezed her eyes, trying to block out the ghastly memory. If it hadn't been for her remaining calm, he would've taken her virginity in a horrific manner.

At gunpoint, she'd donned the wedding gown and went with him to the chapel. However, as his men searched for the minister, she managed to sidle over to the altar to light a candle, then ducked behind it and jumped out of a small window. Too small for Crawford or his men to squeeze through.

She'd had a slight lead on them as she jumped on one of their horses to find the deputy marshal. But the jailhouse stood empty and locked, and she couldn't contact the lawman at home because she didn't know where he lived. Fleeing to the docks had been her second choice.

She had feared for her physical safety and was in

a situation over her head. She shuddered now as she thought of the terror that had pounded through her bones.

She had to get out of this gown. It was turning her stomach.

Willa toweled her face, hung the damp cloth on a wall peg and strode to the door with a new determination fired up inside of her. She had one week to prove herself to her new boss. In fact, the only paying boss she'd ever had in her life.

Harrison slid the crate of liquor bottles from his shoulders, squinting in the blazing sun and trying not to think of the woman he'd just hired. But as he went past the two young delivery men, into the kitchen, past the cooking team of man and wife and to the back storage room, he wondered what and who had brought her to Alaska.

Alaska was a symbol of hope and dreams to many displaced people from around the world. What had Willa been dreaming of, when she'd stepped foot onto this shore?

Seemed everyone who came to Alaska was running from something. Including the drivers, here, two brothers from England who were seeking a less constraining life; the two cooks who'd come from New York to build a business reputation and someday open a restaurant of their own; the accountant in town who'd lost every penny staking a claim in

Dawson only to return to Eagle's Cliff empty-handed and red-faced.

Even Harrison was running to a better life. Better than where he'd grown up, on the poor plains of North Dakota, struggling to make ends meet before and after his parents died. He and his brother, Quinn, now a lawyer in Skagway—in fact, the district attorney—had arrived together in hopes of buying property. It hadn't worked out that way.

Two years ago when they'd landed, they were scammed by the man who was the deputy marshal at that time. Harrison and Quinn had fought hard to rid the land of him and his gangs, but in the process, Harrison had lost two years of his life and his built-up fortune.

He had to start from scratch again, but he wasn't complaining. He cherished every moment the sun shone on his face and every decision he had to make about the tavern.

And what about the woman?

He'd give her an honest shake. One week's time to see how the customers reacted to her and how much hard work she could handle. She seemed healthy and strong enough to last hours on her feet.

But then again, some people were deceptively weak even though they appeared strong.

He was breathing heavily as he stepped from the kitchen back into sunshine and was just lifting the last keg of ale when she sauntered by.

"Gentlemen," she said, nodding to him and the two delivery men.

One of the men swiveled his head so fast he knocked it on the jar of pickled eggs he balanced on his shoulders.

His brawny brother dropped a tray of drinking mugs. Glass rattled.

"Easy," Harrison said, but he could see why the distraction.

Young single women were few and far between.

Harrison, too, followed the gentle sway of her hips and the tantalizing multitude of pearl buttons up her spine that led to the delicate curve of her neck.

It'd been a while since he'd thought of his late wife, Elizabeth. His jaw tensed. Willa and Elizabeth were both the risk-taking kind. Sadly, it had been six years since he'd laid Elizabeth to rest, and he didn't feel much like going over it again.

Harrison took a pencil from his back pocket and approached the shaggy-haired brother. "Where do I sign?"

But the brothers were still staring, mouths agape, watching Willa's every movement as she stepped past the herbs, wiggled past a bench and hopped the two stairs to the boardwalk before she disappeared behind the mercantile.

With a flick of his gloves, Harrison tore the bill out of the younger man's hands and scratched his signature on the bottom.

Willa Banks was inexperienced of men. That much Harrison could tell by the guarded way she'd looked at him and the rigid set of her arms against her bosom.

Still, ignoring her wouldn't be easy.

Chapter Three

"You're going to be the new *bartender?*"

Lily McCloud, owner of Lily's Laces, a friendly woman in her thirties with rich auburn hair, nudged Willa past two racks of colorful dresses to reach the full-length mirror at the back of the shop.

"Yes, ma'am." Willa took a deep breath and stared at her reflection.

The blouse was too fancy with its puffy lace collar, but the split skirt was very functional.

"My goodness. The bartender?" An older lady who smelled like a bakery squeezed in from the aisle and sniffed at Willa.

"With Harrison Rowlan?" A young woman who had the same square jaw as the older one, thereby alerting Willa they must be mother and daughter, clicked her tongue. "You'll be working with Harrison?"

"Mmm-hmm." Willa smoothed the seams on her thighs, trying not to get flustered at the way the women were glaring at her.

"Well, then," Lily drawled in her Texas accent, "you'll be needin' the proper clothing."

"That thing?" The older lady—Willa guessed her to be the baker's wife—with wide-set eyes and hair covered with a netted snood made a face at Willa's skirt.

It was racy for the older folks, Willa thought, split down the middle like it was, mimicking pant legs and four inches off the floor, exposing the ankles of her boots. Bicycle skirts, Lily had called them. The shop owner was wearing one herself. Perhaps it was too modern for the baker's wife, but Willa had seen several young women in Skagway wearing them. It wasn't unusual for someone of Willa's age.

"The job will entail some lifting," Willa explained. "Stretching to reach bottles and glasses. Bending over behind the bar for supplies. A regular skirt isn't as practical."

"Never mind about the skirt. I think it's outrageous," exclaimed the daughter, rubbing her long nose. "You working with Harrison."

Not knowing how to respond, Willa darted a downward glance at Lily, who was kneeling and tugging at the hem. Lily winked at her, making Willa stifle a smile.

"Ladies, if you're done with your selections, I'll have those seams let out tomorrow. Anderson will deliver them in the afternoon."

With another scoff of disapproval at Willa, the baker's wife took her daughter by the elbow and exited through the newly painted pine door.

"Don't let them sway you, honey," said Lily with her southern drawl. "Harrison's the most sought-after bachelor in Eagle's Cliff." She tugged on the hemline. "Ah think the split skirt will do just the trick. You'll need a pair of Levi's denims, too."

"Denim? I've never worn—"

"Ladies can wear them, too. I've got three pair. You can use them when you scrub and polish the bar. Haul supplies from the back, whatever heavy tasks need doing."

"Thank you kindly, but I think not. Not this time." Split skirts were one thing, but denim jeans for women were definitely unusual, even in Alaska, and might draw attention to Willa. She had to be careful.

Thankfully, Lily hadn't made any comments about the dress and burlap shawl Willa had walked in with. Alaska was filled with all sorts of characters in all sorts of financial difficulties. Lily probably figured Willa was in dire straits.

And she figured right.

"You'll also need two regular skirts for more special occasions."

"I'm not sure I need all this clothing. I've only been hired for a week."

"Believe me, honey, you'll be stayin' longer."

Willa swallowed with trepidation and looked into the mirror at Lily. "You think so?"

"Absolutely. Harrison was wise to hire a woman. Clearly, the man's a genius."

Willa couldn't help but like this woman. Unmarried—because Willa saw no wedding ring on her finger—Lily ran the shop the way she wanted to and didn't hesitate to say things that were on her mind.

But Willa wasn't sure about the assumptions with regard to Harrison. He'd been talked in to hiring her, and the deal was only for a seven-day trial.

"Where you from?"

Willa rubbed the back of her neck, stalling for time to think. Truth or no? She found it difficult to confide in anyone—not just her new boss. She opted for the truth. "Montana."

"Always wanted to visit that neck of the woods." A glimmer of gold shone from one of Lily's side teeth. It made her look older than she was, giving her an air of experience.

She went about her tasks selecting two plainer blouses and dark skirts to complement Willa's body shape and skin tone. All a matter of business for the shop owner, but a daunting change of pace for Willa.

If the women she'd just met in the shop were any indication of how the rest of the town might feel,

Willa would be making enemies, as well as friends, in her new position as bartender for the town's most eligible bachelor.

Willa was creating more havoc than Harrison had anticipated.

Crouched beside the bar, his forehead moist with perspiration, he took a crowbar to the crate and plied it open, revealing a dozen bottles of Scotch. He shoved his fist into the loose straw and picked up one of the golden flasks.

A commotion from the kitchen caused him to look up.

"Shoo," came Willa's voice from around the far wall. "Just go home, please. Shoo!"

The rumblings of several male voices followed.

"See you in two days," said one.

"Can't wait till the place opens," said another.

The voices faded and then Willa stepped into the bar.

Harrison, engulfed by the pretty vision, understood immediately what was happening. She'd been escorted home by several men who couldn't part with her company.

She was stunning in her new clothes. A lady's black blouse, pleated at the shoulders, draped softly across her chest. A clinging brown linen skirt accentuated her hips, and a big silver belt buckle cinched her waist. Those long slender legs of hers ended in pointy black boots. His pulse raced in response. She was a lot more female than he was used to seeing.

"I thought…" She fumbled for words. "I thought I would help you unload the crates. Wash some of the mugs in the supply room and polish everything nice and clean behind the bar."

"Yeah," he muttered, suddenly hot.

"Is this where you want me?"

"Yeah."

"Where should I start? The Scotch?"

He nodded. A bead of perspiration trickled down his temple.

"The pots are off the stove, so I suspect the cooks are back. Are they around? I'd like to say hello."

"Yeah." He rubbed his jaw, already bristly although he'd shaved this morning.

"Harrison? Sir? Are you all right?"

Looking at her, he felt as though he'd just gotten a shovel to the chest. She'd combed out her blond hair and it fell against her shoulders, the gold color contrasting with the black blouse and framing her eyes and mouth in such a way that a man couldn't help but notice her.

He tore his gaze off her and commanded his pulse to cool down. "The Abernathys are around here someplace."

"Here we are!"

George and Natalie Abernathy darted out of the

supply room beside the bar, carrying plates and napkins.

Natalie, a rotund woman in her fifties, just as tall and strong as her five-foot-nine husband, set down her supplies. "Pleased to meet you. Harrison tells us you're our new bartender."

Natalie leaned over, her braided rows of dark hair jiggling as she hugged Willa.

Then George pressed forward to shake her hand. Clean-shaven with neatly trimmed white hair, the gent had the cleanest hands Harrison had ever seen on a man. Perfect for a cook. One of the reasons he'd been hired.

"If anyone gives you a rough time," George told her, "you come tell us."

"Thank you." Willa smiled and nodded. The couple were old enough to be her parents. "Where you from?"

"City of New York," said George. "Came for the gold initially, but most of the stakes have already been claimed in the Klondike."

"Just as well," said Natalie. "I prefer cookin' to diggin'."

The three had a laugh over that, while Harrison took a deep breath and wondered how on earth he was supposed to work closely with a woman dressed…so much like a woman.

For God's sake, what was wrong with him?

Natalie admired Willa's clothes. "That's a pretty belt. You think it comes in my size?"

"I imagine," said Willa. "Lily's got everything."

"Harrison told us you went to her shop. Ain't Lily somethin'?"

Natalie picked up her stack of blue-checkered napkins, helped by Willa, and the three made their way to the kitchen. "Lily struck gold last year. Not a huge vein, but enough to build herself a shop this spring."

When they disappeared around the corner, Harrison exhaled his pent-up breath. Lord have mercy, his lungs could work again.

How on earth was he supposed to handle working elbow-to-elbow with a woman who could turn his head so easily? Maybe she wasn't that experienced with men, but he had quite a bit of experience with women and knew when he might be headed for trouble. Unfortunately, he'd already hired her.

Over the course of the next two days as they waited for Friday to arrive, Harrison didn't have any better luck avoiding his new bartender.

Side by side, he showed her the supply rooms and where he kept the stock. He went over the pricings with her, standing at the bar. He preferred to use a drawer than a till, he told her. A drawer wasn't out in the open and so less likely to be a target for thieves. He showed her how to open and close the cash, how to tap the spouts into the kegs to get the ale flowing, how to mix drinks he considered the tavern specials and what sort of behavior was acceptable and unacceptable from the crowd.

"Basically, anything that makes you uncomfortable is not welcome," he told her. "You've got two choices if you feel you're in physical danger. Use the gun beneath the bar. Or holler for me or one of my men. There'll always be a man at the front door to handle unruly customers. Call for Shamus anytime you need him."

"Right," she said.

He wished she'd open up more to him, maybe tell him what was on her mind when he asked about her past, or things she did and didn't like about Alaska.

"I like things fine," she said, but never offered more insight into her character.

Then again, maybe he didn't, either. He found himself unusually quiet when she was near.

He introduced her to Shamus Flannery shortly afterward, a host who would double as a guard—or a bouncer, as some tavern owners called them.

"You know how to use a gun?" Harrison held up the derringer he'd selected especially for her slender hand.

"I was a pretty good shot on the ranch."

"Show me."

He took her out behind the pastures and had her point toward the mountains. She took careful aim, squeezed the trigger and hit the top of the fence he'd instructed her to aim for. Sure enough, she knew how to handle herself.

He took her to the livery stables and showed her where the horses would be boarded, for overnight guests. He introduced her to Billy and Chuck, the two stable hands he'd hired, also skilled gunmen. Harrison only needed one, but due to the gangs roaming Alaska stealing livestock, he'd hired an extra.

The whole time Harrison had spent with Willa, he was conscious of every movement, every sound, every twist of her body and scrape of her shoe.

When she bent across the aisle to pull a cork from a bottle of mead, she accidentally brushed his sleeve.

When she climbed the ladder to wipe the top of the mirror and wash the glass shelves, he was eye level to her thighs.

When she crouched low to the floor to align the kegs of ale, her skirt hems whisked over his cowboy boots and a warm flash of awareness rose up his neck. For a split second, his feet were under her skirts.

As the hours of preparation passed, he wasn't feeling the tension in his blood lower to any significant degree.

What was wrong with him? he wondered again on the eve of their opening night. It was Thursday, past ten o'clock, when he'd thought she'd already retired for the evening, but instead he bumped into her on the balcony just outside her room.

She was leaning against the railing, observing the grand result of all their labor. Her scooped neckline revealed that mesmerizing chain that dangled some-where close to her heart, and he glanced away in haste.

He'd done his best to avoid her around mealtime and especially bedtime, but when he'd come out of his room just now, she'd turned her head and spotted him, so there was no polite way for him to back out.

"Evening," he said awkwardly.

Fumbling, she straightened up to face him and rubbed her hands down the smooth sides of her skirts.

Maybe she wasn't crazy about running into him, either.

"Can't sleep?"

Her eyebrows shot up. "Too excited. Wondering how tomorrow's going to turn out. Lily says it's all everyone's talking about. The grand opening."

He smiled, suddenly much more at ease with the mention of this good news. "Is that so?"

He stepped closer to the rail, close enough that when she whirled around to peer over the bar again, her skirt brushed against his leg.

"Nice to hear, isn't it?" she said. "After all the hard work and planning you've been putting in?"

Below them, the kerosene chandelier glistened off the mirrors. The candles weren't lit, of course, be-cause the bar was closed. But tomorrow he'd have everything up and running.

Eight circular tables with eight chairs apiece filled the bar. Six smaller tables, rectangular and more private, settled in against the farthest wall away from the bar. That would be the dining area for folks who might prefer a quieter table. Maybe Harrison would even get lucky with his business, and a lady or two would show up occasionally. He'd like that. A tamer, calmer place where everyone would feel welcome.

Better for business.

A wall lantern from below lit the path to the kitchen. It was up to him to snuff it every evening. Just like the one behind her head that was creating soft shadows over her shoulders and the warm hollow of her throat.

"You're a man of few words." Her voice was low and rich, as it'd been two days ago when she'd first walked in.

Only two days? It seemed he'd known her for much longer.

"I've always thought actions speak louder than words," he replied.

"Then you speak volumes." Smiling, she leaned over and anchored her warm hand onto his elbow.

Her touch was unexpected.

And there it came again. The knocking of his heart.

She seemed to suddenly be aware of what she'd done, too, for her lips opened as if she was going to apologize, but then thought better of it.

When he turned around to face her full on, she dropped her hand immediately and stared up at him tenderly.

Did she feel the heat of the moment, too?

Did she wonder what it might be like, if he stepped forward and kissed her?

The glow of the lantern behind her left shoulder accentuated the golden shadows of her cheek, the soft rim of her upper lip, the muscles along her throat that flexed and moved with her pulse.

He reached out and cupped her neck, her breath catching as his fingers caressed her warm skin.

Her blouse, a deep chocolate-brown, made her skin glow with health, captured the pink of her lips and dark flecks in her eyes.

If he were a reasonable man, he'd walk away.

If he were reasonable man, he'd say good-night and bid her a pleasant sleep. He'd spin on his boots and saunter down the steps to make sure all the doors were locked securely, with lights out, before going back to settle in his own bed.

But as he looked down into the face of a woman he barely knew, he somehow felt bound to help her escape from the lunatic who'd preyed on her.

Harrison was anchored to the floor. He wasn't going anywhere. He was riveted by the scent of her hair, the color of her skin, the turn of her expression.

This was a woman who begged trouble, he told himself. Who took risks that challenged her life, who was here alone in Alaska, who had problems with matrimony and likely didn't want anything to do with wedding dresses and chapels or men pursuing her. Least of all, her new employer.

If he were a reasonable man, he'd remove his hand from her neck, deny that he pleasured in the way her body felt beneath his touch and cease this connection at once.

But at this moment, his body was telling him…to hell with reason.

Chapter Four

If Willa had known when she'd stepped out of her bedroom this evening that she'd be bumping into Harrison, she never would've ventured out.

When his arms came around her shoulders and he pressed his lips against hers, she was too surprised to move. Or maybe it was the lovely feel of his touch that mesmerized her and rooted her to the planks beneath her high-heeled boots.

It had been a long time since a man had gently kissed her. Several years, in fact, since Jimmy Doe Raven had snuck a kiss behind the games booth at the Montana fairgrounds. She wasn't counting the putrid kiss that Keenan Crawford had planted on her nights ago when he'd pressed a gun to her temples.

This kiss tonight, although unexpected, was not snatched by a wretched thief. She couldn't—

wouldn't—categorize all men in the same dirty league as Crawford.

Something about the vulnerability in Harrison's touch made her feel as though he was a wounded soldier, coming to her arms for comfort. Her body reacted to the physical splendor of being held by a handsome man, the magic tingle of her shoulder blade where the warmth of Harrison's palm seeped into her blouse, the proximity of his heated thigh pressed against hers.

She came alive; she came undone. When his hand came up to touch her cheek, when he roped his fingers into her loose hair, when she felt the soft gasp of surprise at the firmness of his mouth, she responded with the pent-up pressure of a woman who'd never been touched yet ached to know how it might feel. Surely, he was skilled in the bedroom, judging by the assertive way he gripped her, the confidence in his touch, the reaching out and taking of what he wanted at this moment.

Her.

Sliding her mouth against his, she reveled in the friction of contact. Excitement rippled up her stomach. Her breasts felt heavy and constricted in her corset, yearning for release, or perhaps a flittering touch of his fingers.

How would it feel to have a man hold her breasts? This man.

She swallowed hard at the reality of what he was

doing to her. Her mind reeled at the possibilities of where this might lead…how close his bedroom was behind them…how easily they could slip inside and do whatever they wished for however long they wished, without being seen. The other rooms were unoccupied and would be until tomorrow.

The thought of being with Harrison sent her pulse thundering over a cliff. The feverish pitch between them grew hotter and his touch bolder. He pressed his leg closer and gripped her waist tighter, whispering, "Willa…what are you doing to me?"

The shock of his voice brought her to her senses. She was here in Alaska in order to survive. In order to overcome every man who'd ever tried to take over her life.

This wasn't what she wanted. Another man to control her. To tell her what to do.

And fear—plain cold fear—that he would try to overtake her as Crawford had, made her react harshly. Her mind told her Harrison and Crawford were not the same, but an image of Crawford swallowed her logic and she reacted in self-defense. She pressed her fingers into Harrison's elbows, pushed hard and broke free.

He was breathing deeply as he searched her face. His dark eyes misted in the soft kerosene lamplight. The line of his jaw twitched. He swiped at his mouth, rough from their kiss, and stepped back against the rail.

"I'm sorry."

She fought to catch her breath. "So am I. That should never have happened."

"Of course. I…I apologize."

Anger rumbled up her throat. At being forced by Crawford to squirm in her own bed, and at now being taken for granted by Harrison, a man she'd known for even less time than Crawford. This man was her employer. Supposed to be her protector.

She tried to squelch her rising indignation, tried to tell herself maybe she was to blame by being out here alone in the middle of the night, by making herself available to an eligible bachelor who'd likely had scores of women in his past.

No, she reasoned. It wasn't her fault. Just as it hadn't been her fault with the butcher. "I didn't ask for this."

"I was completely out of line. I want you to feel safe in this place."

It was too late for that. She didn't feel safe at all. Not in the tavern, not here just outside her bedroom and definitely not alone with this man.

With her heart thumping against her ribs, her muscles heavy with the rush of fear, she picked up her skirts and turned on her heels. It took every ounce of restraint not to break into a run to her room. When she got past the door, she slammed it closed and secured the latch with a loud click, hoping with all her might that he got the message.

* * *

Harrison closed his eyes in embarrassment at the loud click of the latch. It echoed in the still night and underscored Willa's decree.

Stay away from me.

Here she was, trying to flee a crazed man from Skagway and instead she wound up straight in the arms of another stranger. Him!

It wasn't like Harrison to take advantage.

He rubbed his mouth and took the stairs down to the kitchen. He checked the lock on the back door, snuffed the lanterns on the way back up to his bedroom and reminded himself he'd overstepped the boundaries of propriety by kissing her like that. Maybe she'd been through more difficulty with that would-be groom of hers than she was willing to confide. In addition, Harrison suspected she was a virgin. The bottom line was she deserved more respect from him.

In the privacy of his room, surrounded by dressers of newly cut pine, he unbuttoned his shirt and slid out of it. Cool air from the open window filtered in, lifting the heat from his chest and dampening the sweat of his brow. What was it about her that pulled him to the edge? That caused the ripple in his skin, caused him to hesitate when he breathed around her, quickened his senses and made his thoughts reel in confusion?

She was his bartender, and she'd have to prove her

worth tomorrow. He was unaccustomed to working so closely with a woman, he told himself, that's why he was so aware of her whenever she brushed by.

He sank onto the mattress and slid one long leg out of his pants, then the other.

"What kind of person am I? Can't even let the woman do her work."

Feeling unseasonally warm, he stood in the night breeze, naked, flattening his hands on the window-sill and studying the vast expanse of the mountains in the distance.

Moonlight skimmed the meadows, highlighting the forests filled with scrub pines and glistening willows. Purple fireweed cascaded down the slopes, and he could well imagine the nocturnal animals rummaging through the leaves. The white cliff, from where the town got its name, glistened in the glow of the moon. Trees rose high above the cliffs, half a dozen filled with huge nests made of sticks and straw and leaves, where bald eagles soared above the ocean. He couldn't see them at this distance, but he knew they were there, as they always were in the quiet of the night.

Life never seemed to be simple anymore. It was once, when he was younger and never thought past tomorrow. But that had ended abruptly the night he'd lost Elizabeth.

The memory thudded in his heart. Then the memories of other difficult things that had followed.

Getting to Alaska. Being wrongfully accused of robbery and murder. Clearing his name. Starting over from scratch with his tavern. Hiring a woman he knew hardly anything about.

He would aim for simple once more. She was the hired help. Tomorrow, and the days that followed, he wouldn't step any closer to her than necessary.

A blast of warm air billowed the right side of the curtains and rolled over his chest, tugging at the small hairs. The hard muscles in his arms tightened.

He rubbed the scars over the left side of his ribs. The area was growing less tender, although the knife wound would always show. It had happened two months ago when he'd stepped into the path of an oncoming blade that was intended for an innocent woman, a mother who'd been protecting her adolescent daughters from being attacked by vigilantes. His brother, Quinn, had been with him on the trail, and protecting the woman and her family had been done in the line of duty, as Harrison and Quinn were trying to clear their names as well as protect the lives of other innocent victims on the trail.

As for Willa, Harrison had to stop thinking about her. He had a tavern to run and it was opening tomorrow.

"Hey, Harrison, open the doors. We'd like to order an ale from that new wench of yours!"

Willa heard the calls coming through the tavern

doors as she came down the stairs the next evening at five-thirty, a good half hour before they were set to open. Doing up the last button of her cuffs, she peered over at the two barmaids and frowned with curiosity.

"Ma'am." Sarah O'Grady, a former farm girl from Minnesota with red braids who was a couple of years older than Willa, lined up a row of sparkling drinking glasses on the side of the bar. "They've been hollerin' for the past ten minutes."

"There's a lineup," declared her older sister, Rosa, forty pounds heavier and just as pretty.

"What?" Willa raced to the windows. She pulled up the blinds, letting in a stream of evening sunshine. Two dozen male heads turned to gaze at her from the street. Instead of looking away shyly, Willa planted her hands on her hips and smiled back. "Well, indeed there is."

Several men cheered. Others whistled. The ones in the front clapped.

Whatever nervousness had flitted through her today, as she and the staff had worked toe-to-toe, dissipated.

Customers had come.

"We'll be right with you, fellas!" Willa waved and the hooting and hollering continued.

"Broken chair is fixed." Shamus slid in from the kitchen, carrying the slat-back chair whose leg had needed realigning, and set it down near the back.

Natalie followed, setting a stack of menus down for Shamus to arrange by the door.

The only two people missing from the bar were Natalie's husband, George, and Harrison. Willa was aware they were both working somewhere in the back rooms. She could hear the muted voice of Harrison as he called to the men at the back door of the kitchen to unload last-minute ale that had just come in on the ships this afternoon.

Pivoting toward the bar, Willa felt her split skirt flutter at her boots. She raced behind the sleek wooden slab. Her black split skirt, ruffled brown blouse and feminine leather boots were not only comfortable, but also rather pleasing to the eye.

Of course, her outfit wasn't as dramatic as the sisters'. Their blouses were more clingy, with bodices that tucked under their breasts, fabric that cinched their waists and gently flowing A-line skirts. More classy than provocative, to which Willa gave Harrison credit. He wasn't aiming to make the tavern an alcohol-guzzling, rough-and-tumble drinking hole, but something of restraint and neighborly charm.

Bending down behind the bar, Willa reached for her lineup of liquors to display on the counter. The derringer Harrison had hidden on a rear shelf glinted at her. She ignored it in her rush to work.

She thought she might have a bit of time to ease into her duties tonight, but the evening looked to be busy. She laid out a linen tea towel and put out what she figured would be the most popular brands. Mead and malt from the United Kingdom, rye from the Canadian wheat fields, vodka from Russia, whisky from Glasgow, bourbon from Kentucky and wines from the new vineyards of California. Beers came from all over the States, particularly Philadelphia, which supplied Harrison's favorite brews.

He'd told her the mahogany bar was imported from Philadelphia, too, and he'd come across it by accident three weeks ago in Skagway when a steamer was unloading it and looking for a sale, along with the chairs and tables he'd bought from other ships that day.

Philadelphia, it seemed, had a reputation for great beers and taverns.

With a smile, she surveyed her stock. The wheel of kerosene lights hanging over the bar glittered in the mirror beside her. She glanced up at her reflection and everything looked in order—hair tied loosely at the back with a bow, blouse straight and neatly buttoned, necklace glistening off her chest. In the mirror, she also caught sight of Harrison leaning against a far wall, watching her.

Her skin flushed with heat at the way he was assessing her. His dark eyes somber, his stance cool and exacting, strong arms crossed against his chest as if he were holding back his thoughts.

Did he have faith in her? Did he believe she could do this tonight?

Lord, she hoped he'd forgotten how she'd pushed

him away last night. Not that she was sorry she'd done so, only that she'd done it with much more strength and anger than she'd intended. She was thinking of Crawford when she'd pushed Harrison.

He didn't seem the type of man who needed to be harshly treated to get the message that she wasn't interested in his advances.

With a flicker of her eyes in his direction, she turned away from the mirror and took a step toward her bill drawer. Sliding it out, she made one last check that she'd have change to give out, and that blank receipts, along with a sharpened pencil, were stacked neatly at the side for the dinner bills.

Her muscles tensed, unsure of what the evening would bring, but knowing that it had already brought a welcome change from her stifling life in Montana.

"Open the doors, Shamus," Harrison called from his stance against the wall. Just as calm and quiet as if it were any other day of the week.

Shamus complied. "Welcome, folks, welcome."

He propped the door open on its peg. The crowd strode in, some removing their hats, some being escorted to tables by Sarah and Rosa and some coming straight to the bar for Willa.

"Pour me a Guinness, miss." The banker tossed his hat to the slick countertop.

"And me a shot of bourbon," said a man introducing himself as the town baker, Festus Whittler.

Willa slid the mug of ale to the banker, then grabbed the bottle of bourbon. "I've met your wife and daughter, Mr. Whittler."

The sun-beaten crags in his cheeks clenched. "Have you now? Then I'd be pleased if you don't mention I dropped in here tonight."

She nodded. For some men, visiting the local tavern was a secret, she supposed. She had to remember that her duty was to serve and not ask questions.

"How much'll that be?" A robust man in a miner's hat squeezed through the throng, pointing to the shot glasses.

"Forty cents a shot."

"I pay twenty in Detroit."

"You're standing in Alaska, sir."

Other men around him chuckled, but Willa stood firm with her gaze.

"Gimme two!" called another man.

The miner grumbled and sat down. "Name's Eli. Pour me a shot. Maybe your pretty hand will bring me luck in striking gold."

His comment seemed to stick with the others. "Gimme me some luck over here," cried the baker beside him, followed by a table of businessmen sitting at the front window.

Others called out. "Pour me a drink and let's see if your hand brings in any supplies from Seattle. I've been waiting on a boat of fencing for six weeks!"

"I'll take a glass of mead for some luck with lady love!"

Laughter followed the last comment, and Willa cheerfully obliged them all.

She was aware of Harrison watching her as he greeted guests and recommended tavern drinks and dinner specials. He moved smoothly to wherever he was needed—carting kegs from the back, moving chairs, helping guests with their luggage up the stairs.

She didn't notice the time flying by, but the light coming in from the windows turned pitch-dark, the lights above them twinkled brighter, meals were served by Sarah and Rosa, and in some cases when they got too busy to juggle everything, Natalie herself brought out plates loaded with breaded fish, braised rabbit legs, turtle soup, corn bread and goose with turnips.

At some point when it seemed Willa had barely moved from her spot, her elbows flying with the orders, the drawer slamming in and out from the receipts she collected from Sarah and Rosa, she noticed Harrison had slipped in beside her at the bar to help fill some glasses.

Did he not think she could handle it herself? Could he not see she was coping quite well?

His sleeve brushed hers as he leaned over to pour a shot of rye, but she was also reaching for it at the same time, so her fingers accidentally slid over his on the neck of the bottle.

Their eyes locked. Her stomach rattled.

Eli, the miner from Detroit, called out in good humor, "Business is so good they don't have enough hands to deal it all."

"They have enough hands," the baker responded to the laughter. "But not enough bottles!"

The side of Harrison's mouth tugged up at her in pleasure. "Ladies first."

He dropped his hand, her fingers followed his, then she quickly regained her rhythm and continued pouring, slamming and collecting money.

Well into the evening, Harrison nudged up beside her and whispered in her ear. "Take a break. You've been on your feet for four hours."

"Four already? Goodness. But so have you."

"Take a break, Willa."

Willa glanced up to the room. The faces were changing, but the place remained packed.

Rosa was singing, strumming on a banjo and propped on a stool at the back, a spot where Harrison hoped to bring in a piano that was on order from Seattle. The song was pretty, her voice amazingly loud and vibrant. The men were awed by her, judging by the stricken faces.

Other men had started up a game of poker— actually, two—at the rear tables. The dining tables were still packed. Lord, Willa didn't think the town of Eagle's Cliff had this many men.

And so many of them watching her.

"Thanks," she said to Harrison. Oddly, she didn't feel uncomfortable around him when they talked about work. It was only the private stuff that was difficult to handle.

She slid out from the bar, ducked down the hall, made a stop at the privy and returned to the kitchen. She nodded to the husband-and-wife cooks who were slowing down somewhat but still preparing meals. Willa poured herself a glass of water and guzzled.

"Sandwich?" Natalie used a big knife and board to slice corned beef.

"Oh, yes. Just a bite."

"Sit." Natalie brought her a plate.

Willa chomped on the heavenly rye, and the side pickle, rolling around the flavor on her tongue. "It's delicious. No wonder Harrison hired you."

George chuckled, sliding dirty plates into the soapy bucket by the window. "A lot of these customers came to see you."

Willa tried but couldn't stifle the moment of pleasure. "I was hoping that might happen. But novelty wears off quick. The trick is to keep them coming back for more."

She leaped up off the chair, thanked the cooks for the meal and made her way back to the bar.

At the end of the hall, however, she came face-to-face with a rough-looking character in his thirties who hadn't shaved for several days and wasn't walking straight.

He wobbled toward her. "Hey, pretty lady."

Before she could respond, he lunged at her, one hand hitting her shoulder, the other hand pawing her breast.

"Ahh!" she screamed and kicked his shin, her pulse pounding at a crazy speed.

He cussed, stumbled backward, and in an instant, Harrison was there. He yanked the man's arm behind his back and dragged him down the hall and out the front of the bar.

Willa, stunned, took a moment to breathe. *Calm down.* It wasn't Crawford, she told herself. She was safe.

She gathered her composure, afraid of the commotion this situation might make, but Harrison was very discreet, nodding to Shamus to give the man a good talking-to outside. Shamus did as was asked, and Willa returned to the busy bar, but never got a chance to thank Harrison till after one o'clock when the bar closed and he locked the door behind the last customer.

George and Natalie were in the kitchen, cleaning up. Sarah and Rosa were hauling away dirty dishes and wiping down tables.

Shamus pulled down the front blinds of the tavern, shook hands with Harrison and bid her a good-night as he strolled out.

"Great tally at the bar, Willa," Shamus hollered.

She smiled and gave him a friendly wave goodbye.

Willa would likely be the last to leave tonight,

for she had to soap up the last of the drinking glasses and dry them.

Harrison approached her, a mountain of a man, and yet he seemed to be as alert and energetic now as he'd been at the beginning of the evening. "Some of that can wait till morning, if you're tired."

"I prefer to finish now. So we have a fresh slate tomorrow. How many guests registered?" Shamus had taken care of signing them in.

"All rooms are filled."

She smiled lightly.

Harrison moved in next to her and pulled out the cash drawer. "More than I expected."

Finally. A word from the boss about her performance.

She dunked another glass into the basin, trying not to show her delight.

"You surprise me, Willa."

The sound of her name rumbled low off his lips. Shamus had snuffed out all the kerosene lanterns except the two on the wall behind her, and the soft lighting slanted against the curve of Harrison's lean cheek and ropey sinews of his neck. His thick dark hair, slicked back at his temples, glistened in the shadows.

"How so?" She spread a tea towel out on the bar and lined up the neat row of mugs.

"For one, my feet are sore. I imagine yours don't feel any better."

A smile tugged at the corner of her mouth. "My boots are well worn, so I didn't get any new blisters. But I confess the balls of my feet are sore."

"Two, I didn't expect a lineup before the doors opened."

"Sure you did."

His eyebrows shot up.

She wiped the counter clean. "Otherwise you wouldn't have hired me."

"Maybe I was hoping for it, but I wasn't expecting it."

Gentle laughter bubbled out of her.

"And three, I can't believe how hard you can work."

"For a woman?"

"Well…"

"If I were a man, you wouldn't be complimenting me on my stamina, would you?"

"I suppose not." He looked to the jar that held her gratuities. Halfway through the night, she had to change it from a regular glass to a tall mug. Some men had been so generous they'd left bills. There were even three gold nuggets inside.

His gaze trailed hers to the money.

"I believe I've earned more in one night here than I could've in a month of working full-time at the dress shop."

"Then you're staying," he said.

Taken aback by the comment, she let her hand rest

on the counter next to his. He thought she might be leaving? The thought had never occurred to her that he'd be concerned she might go.

She looked up into his eyes, noting how the brown flecks glimmered in the golden light, feeling her stomach tighten and her throat squeeze as he waited for her reply. She was brought back to last night when they were alone on the balcony, how his kiss had felt and the firmness of his hand on the back of her waist. Was this moment leading to a kiss, too?

Chapter Five

~~~

She was tempting, thought Harrison as he stared down into the sophisticated warmth of Willa's eyes. His pulse rumbled through his body, quaking like a tide, challenging him to dip lower and press his lips against hers.

He noticed everything about her at once. The spill of blond hair tossed to one side, the soft perfect angle of her jaw, the slight flare of her nostrils as she fought to catch her breath.

The ruffle of fabric down her blouse captured the swell of her bosom, molding to her slender waistline. The skirt she wore tonight, split down the center like it was, pronounced the pretty shape of her hips and thighs.

But it was more than physical, the things he noticed about Willa Banks.

She'd been so much more than he'd expected

tonight, this stranger who'd walked in off the street and demanded that he hire her. The woman whose looks were as supple as deerskin, but her character as hard as an anvil when it came to delivering drinks and standing up to men twice her height and weight.

Swallowing past the desire that lumped in his throat, Harrison lowered his hands to the wash bucket she'd finished with behind the counter, accidentally brushing his knuckles against hers and setting his heart skidding in another direction unknown.

Dammit, it wasn't safe to be around her. He didn't like the feeling of being slightly out of control. He preferred his old self. Calm, confident, certain of who he was and what he wanted out of his life for the next little while. He wanted to build his business and come to know the folks in town, since he hadn't stayed in one place for the past two years of being in Alaska and hadn't gotten to know anyone to any great depth. He wanted to get to know the women, too, on friendly, casual terms. It wasn't like him to fall for the first pretty face he saw.

But he *wasn't* falling for her. This was a ridiculous train of thought.

"You're done with his?" His deep voice hummed through the night air as he indicated the soapy bucket.

Flustered, she pushed at the bands of hair behind her ear and blinked at the water.

She was flustered, too. Why?

"Yes," she said. "Of course. Thank you."

Effortlessly, he lifted the liquid, turned on his cowboy boots and made his way to the kitchen.

She didn't follow him. He didn't hear any movements from her and didn't strain to find out what she was doing next as he opened the back door and emptied the water in the drainage ditch of the garden. Didn't see her when he came back in and tossed the bucket into the corner. Didn't care to think about how quickly she disappeared when he snuffed out the final lantern and trudged up the stairs to his own bed.

He was through with building relationships with women, with the prospect of anything permanent with the fairer sex. Had been for the past six years of his life.

"You better goddamn find her."

Keenan Crawford stood in the cold back room of his Skagway butcher shop in the hour before the store opened and spoke to one of his most trusted men.

Crawford picked up the meat saw, angled the carcass of pork on the table before him and sawed through the ribs. Cold raw flesh squeezed through his stubby fingers. The rip of the blade calmed his nerves. It was this slicing ritual that always settled him in the mornings when he was troubled by something. It cleared his mind and gave him a chance to think on business—what private orders to give to his secret gang of men.

Owen Price, guns holstered and always ready for

trouble, paced the floor. "Dooley's making another check at the docks."

"It's been four days since she disappeared. Give me answers. Not a description of who's doin' what." The rumble of Crawford's words echoed off the cement walls of the room known as the cooler. Ice blocks insulated the perimeter.

"Yes, sir."

Crunch went the saw as Crawford hit bone. "Dammit. You're makin' me lose my concentration." He readjusted the ribs and the blade went through flesh as soft as cream.

As he recalled the night of humiliation, a blinding heat seeped up through his chest and settled at the base of his thick neck. The rage dampened the sweat on his temples and soaked the armpits of his shirt. Yet, his fists, as red and meaty as the flesh he handled, remained steady on the pork.

There were two pressing reasons why he needed Mary Somerset back.

First, he truly pleasured in the way the curves of her flesh had felt, pressed beneath his, when he'd forced her to put on the wedding gown. He shouldn't have waited to nail her. He should have bedded her right there and then, but that was his fault for believing her and her promises of a remarkable wedding eve.

He grit his teeth. It wouldn't happen again.

Second, she might've overheard something she

shouldn't have, that morning when she'd come into his shop while he was speaking privately to his men.

How much had she heard of their plans to convene that night and steal the cattle? How he was driving up the price of beef by carefully controlling when they released it on the black market?

She hadn't been jittery or anything afterward, so she may not have realized the intent of the conversation. He'd quickly tried to cover it up by remarking on her body, which seemed to anger her. Hadn't she liked the attention he gave her? The devotion he'd shown by choosing her, above all others?

He couldn't take the chance to let her go. It was either make her his wife—knowing that a wife couldn't testify against a husband, and where he'd be close enough to strike the fear of God into her if she so much as breathed a word about him—or ensure she'd never be around to make anyone else a wife.

If he had to get rid of her, it would be a goddamn waste of beautiful flesh. He snarled, "What right does she have to walk away from me?"

"None, sir." Price's eyes flickered in fear.

Didn't every single woman in town believe Crawford would make a fine husband? Blast them all to hell, he was the richest man in town!

He spat a wad of chewing tobacco at the dirt floor. It splattered next to the others.

Richest man in town and he couldn't tell a soul. What satisfaction was there in that?

He had some competition for the position, but that just made his financial accomplishments all the greater. Sure, the casinos that dotted Skagway brought in fistfuls of gold for their owners, and so did some of the supply ships for the captains who were bright enough to recognize the bonanza that Alaska was.

But what about him?

When the hell would he be able to announce his brilliance?

There was a shortage of meat in Alaska and hadn't he rigged it so that all imported supplies for the district came through the harbor to him? Didn't he attend the livestock auctions scattered through the valleys and follow the pathway of nearly every horse and cow through Alaska?

His occupation gave him the insight and opportunity to steal whatever he wanted.

He dealt illicitly in trading stolen horses and selling them as pack animals, and selling stolen beef at the going black-market price. And no one in Alaska had any inkling that the mastermind behind it all, the millionaire, was the kindly butcher down the street.

Wasn't he the savior of hungry men and women on the trail?

A goddamn hero is what he was!

Yet he couldn't brag to anyone. His men knew what he did but even they didn't know the extent of his riches. Like his dearly departed mama—the most successful madam who ever owned a brothel in New Orleans—told him when she'd trained him in the cutthroat ways of the world, he couldn't trust a soul but himself.

The private back door squeaked open. Crawford glanced up at the two men who entered. Two skinny cousins by the names of Dooley and Tyrone Younger. Due to the shameful look on their faces, Crawford reacted with a blast of fury.

He picked up the loaded rifle propped by the door, his hands still bloody from the pork.

"Don't you tell me," he growled at Tyrone, pointing the barrel at the shaking mouth, "that no one sighted her on the ships."

Just because Harrison was through with women in a serious sense didn't mean he didn't enjoy being with them.

"Evening." Harrison tipped his hat to the three pretty ladies who gathered outside his tavern. Perfume saturated the air. "Let me get the door for you."

"Nice to see you again, Harrison," cooed the baker's daughter, Morgan. Colorful red ribbons adorned her hair.

In a cloud of blue-checkered fabric, her friend Stella batted her long lashes. "We're just coming in for a bite to eat. I heard the breaded cod is out of this world."

"Will you be serving us, Harrison?" Cora, the

clerk from the bank smiled up at him, her freckles gleaming in the late-evening sunshine.

He grinned. "I'll leave that to Shamus and the ladies. But I'll drop by your table to see how you're doing."

Morgan's cheeks dimpled with pleasure, Cora shrugged her rounded shoulders with a flirtatious tilt to her head and Stella pursed her lips with appreciation.

He followed them inside to the crowded, buzzing tavern. The place was already packed and it was only six-thirty. He was just coming back from speaking with one of his suppliers and the meeting had taken longer than he'd expected.

Harrison nodded to the bouncer. "Shamus, please take care of these ladies. Drinks are on me tonight."

"Yes, sir."

With another friendly nod to the giggling gals, Harrison headed for the back. He caught Willa's curious gaze from behind the bar and felt his breath tighten.

No, sir, he had nothing to feel guilty about. He still savored the banter with all women and the possibility of courtships. What would be wrong with a midnight stroll by the bay? He hadn't had much time in the past two years, but Eagle's Cliff was proving to be bountiful in the number of women catching his eye.

That's the reason he attributed to his attraction to Willa. Just a passing fancy and welcome reintroduction into a normal life after two years of being chased through the valleys of Alaska, clawing his way up the mountains on foot, hiding along riverbanks to avoid wrongful conviction. Fighting for those on the trail who'd been robbed blind, and in some cases, their family members killed by outlaws.

Hell, what red-blooded man wouldn't be attracted to *every* woman he met after coming out of that purgatory?

There was safety in numbers. The more women he courted, the safer he'd be. Not that he had anything against marriage. Hell, he'd be the first to congratulate one of his friends if he bit the bullet, but it was just that Harrison's frame of mind hadn't been there for six years.

Too much heartache involved.

Elizabeth. She popped into his misty thoughts, just like that. He frowned and lowered his gaze to the floor.

He ducked out to the hallway, washed up and re-entered the room.

Taking a deep breath, he stepped behind the bar to join Willa. He worked wherever an extra pair of hands could help, and for the past week since they'd opened, mostly he was needed behind the bar.

He poured a Scotch, added chips of ice that Willa had scraped off an ice block earlier in the day and slid the drink to the whiskered old guy at the counter.

"I've got to hand it to you, Willa," Harrison drawled above the buzz of the crowd. "Your first week in is impressive. Packed crowds from open to close."

Pouring a whisky sour, she raised her eyebrows and smiled. "Glad you approve, sir."

"Sir?"

She shrugged, eyes twinkling, and whisked around him as nimble as a ballet dancer on a polished hardwood floor.

"Your one week is up," he told her.

Her skirts stopped twirling. She turned around, squeezing between the drawers and the lip of the bar top, mere inches away. Her amused expression faded from her face as she waited for the verdict.

He didn't mean to prolong it. "I'd like you to stay on."

"I'm hired? Permanent?"

"Yes, ma'am."

"Ma'am?"

"It counterbalances the 'sir.'"

Her gentle expression gave way to a cheerfulness he hadn't seen in her since she'd arrived. "I'd be happy to work for you, Harrison."

The words took a bigger chunk out of his heart than he anticipated. It was just a job, he told himself.

Rosa, the barmaid, squeezed in behind the bar and nudged Willa's elbow, ending the spell. "How's about somethin' sweet and alcoholic for the ladies at the far end?" Rosa pointed to the female customers Harrison had escorted in.

Willa's forehead grooved with concern. "Are they all over twenty-one?"

Rosa chuckled. "Oh, God, yes."

"Then I know just the thing." Willa turned away from Harrison and concentrated on her cocktails.

He watched in fascination as she mixed peach juice, raspberry syrup, white rum, a sprinkle of cinnamon and a few other ingredients into a silver cocktail shaker.

It smelled good. "What's that?"

She put the lid on and shook. "One of my own creations. I call it the Alaskan Mule."

He laughed. Maybe it was the serious edge to her expression, or maybe it was the name of the drink and who the recipients were, but Willa was highly amusing.

One of the customers at the bar, an old gent, slid his empty mug to Harrison. "Refill, please."

Harrison caught the mug with a slap, poured more ale into the dimpled glass and slid it back.

Customers pulled Harrison and Willa in different directions for the next several hours. Banjo music played in the background. Food orders needed to be brought back and forth from the kitchen, and Rosa and Sarah couldn't keep up, so Willa helped where she could. She was pure business. All the time. She never seemed to even notice she was in the same room with him. And she never, ever, spoke about anything more personal than how they were getting low on Scotch.

Dammit.

Harrison turned his head toward the stairs and lunged to assist Shamus with three new guests checking in. They needed help with luggage and instructions on how and where to board their horses. One old-timer dragged in a crate of rabbits. The hopping ears produced several chuckles from the crowd.

"Let's haul these outside, shall we?" Harrison asked. He delivered the rabbits to the stables himself and came back in time to seat another party of eight.

Harrison didn't have any more private conversations with Willa that evening, much to his frustration. Nor the next one. But the day after that, Sunday, their day of rest, he bumped into her unexpectedly on the boardwalk behind the ice-cream parlor.

He was on his way to the bay to speak to the fishermen about buying more salmon.

"Oh," she said with a blush. "Harrison." She'd just scooped some chocolate ice cream into her mouth from a tin bowl.

"You alone?" He looked behind her to the alleyway. Two other customers were carrying bowls of ice cream, but they were sauntering off in another direction.

Staring up at him, Willa licked the chocolate off her lips. In a stunning yellow gown with square neckline plunging to her cleavage, she radiated femininity.

A knot formed in his gut, one that came quite often when he stood next to her, one that made him waver in his decision of whether to be with her, or to continue on his way.

"I was visiting with Lily, but she had to go work on a dress that's due tomorrow. So I'm alone, yes."

There was a glow about her skin. Or maybe it was her eyes. A softness and allure he couldn't resist.

Forget about the fishermen. Who wanted to spend time with a bunch of weathered old men when he could have the buoyant company of Willa?

"May I join you for a scoop?"

Her dark eyes skimmed past his shoulders toward the ocean. "I was just…just heading to the water to watch the birds."

He saw it in her eyes. The hesitation, the careful summation of his motives.

He swallowed hard at the honesty of her emotions, but it didn't prevent his gut from slamming hard in disappointment. Then he chastised himself for wanting more.

"And you don't relish any company," he said softly.

Chapter Six

⁂

"No." Willa coughed. "No, no," she spluttered, trying to say something polite to Harrison. "Please join me."

What else could she say? He was staring down at her in expectation, and he was her employer.

It's just that this was her only day off after a long week of proving herself at the tavern, and she wanted to relax and discover the town of Eagle's Cliff. She didn't want to be on guard, wondering what he might do next, wondering if she was saying the right thing or being polite enough or witty enough or enough of anything.

They'd been getting on quite well the past couple of days, a sisterly-brotherly sort of companionship.

At least, it was that way from afar.

Now, standing next to him and staring up into the depths of his brown eyes, watching the sunlight graze his firm chin and smooth upper lip, she didn't feel so sisterly toward him.

Her stomach did that flop it always seemed to do around him, and her warning bells pitched to high alert.

Every time he stepped near, her skin rippled with warning, she braced herself for the possibility that he'd probe into her past, and he just plain smelled too good.

He was still staring at her, his dark eyes swirling with trouble, the corner of one lip tilted up with mischief and the wisp of a breeze blowing through his dark hair.

"I'm probably the last person you want to spend time with. On your only day off."

"Don't be silly." Trying to temper her racing pulse, she dipped her spoon into her delicious ice cream. "What's your favorite flavor?"

"That looks good." His eyes twinkled. "Can I get you anything else while I'm in there?"

She shook her head. He scooted into the parlor and a minute later came out with two scoops of his own.

He pressed a steady hand to the small of her back and steered her toward the ocean. The unexpected move made her catch her breath.

The spot where he touched felt uncomfortably hot and she wiggled away.

"You okay?" He looked down at her flustered expression.

She gulped her chocolate. "Itchy skin."

His lashes flickered. "Ah."

The hot afternoon sun blazed down the boardwalk, cutting the planks in two with a crisp shadow line. Her long skirts ruffled as she walked. She squirmed in the prickly heat while he strode comfortably in the coolness. If she were walking alone, she'd have the shade to herself, another reason why it was a mistake to invite him along.

"Whereabouts in Montana are you from?"

She jolted with the question. Probing, probing. Here it came. "The north."

"The only place I know is Billings."

"That so."

"Are you close to Billings?"

"Not anymore." She laughed gently.

"It's beautiful country. The mountains and all those trees."

She nodded. "Alaska reminds me of Montana. Except for the added beauty of the ocean."

She wasn't about to disclose anything significant. It might endanger her position here, hiding from Crawford. Besides, her former life with her uncles and cousins was private business. Harrison should keep his nose out of her affairs. Not that she meant to be rude, only protective.

"Maybe you think I'm being nosy." He glanced down at her revealing neckline and she was suddenly aware of the view he must have.

"Not at all," Willa told him, trying to find some

pleasure in being trapped with him, but only feeling worse. "You're just being neighborly."

"How did your family react when you told them you were heading to Alaska?"

Heat flushed through her jaw. "This ice cream is absolutely incredible. They have no shortage of customers at the ice-cream parlor."

"They didn't take it well, I guess."

"Would you look at that sailing ship? The sheer size, my goodness."

She peered out to the ocean, at the shimmering flat water that filled the natural U-shape of the harbor. Two schooners sailed the seas. Seagulls cawed overhead. Three magnificent bald eagles—with their white-feathered heads from which they'd gotten their name—that normally nested on the white cliff sailed high overhead, almost touching the fluffy white cloud, it seemed to Willa.

She smiled in delight at spotting them, and Harrison followed her gaze upward. They shared the seconds of splendor before the eagles soared around the cliffs and disappeared.

"Or maybe your family supported your move," Harrison continued, as if the conversation had never stopped. His wide shoulders blocked the sun. "I don't have any family left, save for my brother Quinn who lives in Skagway. Either way, I've always taken for granted that I can come and go as I please. As a man, I mean. Wherever in the world I want to head, I just pack my bags and don't ask permission. But since I've come to Alaska...I've appreciated women more."

The handsome creases at his eyes doubled as he chose his words carefully, trying to share something personal, it seemed, a personal thought on a sensitive subject. "It's not so easy to travel alone, I imagine. Men clawing at you. Expecting you to stay...in the position they think you should be in."

She was silent. Wanting to say so much more, but too afraid to reveal herself, the intimate parts of her thoughts. Maybe he'd laugh at her, as her cousins had.

His gaze flickered over her quiet face. With a gentle tug of his lips, in an emotion she couldn't quite read, he finished his last scoop of ice cream.

"Well, I won't bother you anymore. Obviously, you'd like to be alone." He turned to leave.

"Harrison," she whispered, flooded with shame for ignoring him and his questions.

But it was too late to speak privately, for they were suddenly surrounded by women. Six or seven of them, all eating ice cream.

Come to gaze at Harrison, no doubt.

"Willa," they shouted, surprising her. One of the gals stepped forward. "May I talk to you please? My boss at the mercantile refuses to up my wages and I thought you could advise me. I went to Lily first, but she's busy sewing a new jacket for Mrs. Whittler, and suggested I talk to you." The young lady glanced in

Harrison's direction and lowered her voice when she turned back to Willa. "You might give me advice on how to wrangle a raise out of the cheapskate."

"And me," shouted another young woman. "They've brought me here by ship to be a school-teacher, yet the town's businessmen refuse to pay equal wages to a man."

Harrison stepped past Willa toward the board-walk stairs.

Alarmed, she whispered into his shoulder. "I didn't tell them anything about my pay."

"I suppose," he said with an amused dimple in his dark cheek, "they figured it out on their own. Looks like you're a hero. Go ahead and give them some pointers."

Pointers? Her?

"Ladies," he said to a sea of feminine laughter, "arm yourselves well, but not too well. Take it easy on us men."

He dipped his broad shoulders and edged out of the crowd. In a final look back, he playfully saluted Willa.

She didn't feel like a hero. She felt like a heel the way she'd treated him. But even that was too late to correct, for two ladies scooted to either side of him, cupped their arms under his elbows and tugged him toward the ocean.

That's where *she* was supposed to go with Harrison. He'd asked if he could take a stroll with *her*.

He didn't seem to be missing her company. One of the young ladies bobbed her head toward his, said something, and he responded with deep laughter.

A wave of disappointment filtered through Willa. He'd wanted to spend a little time together by the ocean and what had she done? She might as well have slapped him in the face, for all the conversation she'd contributed.

In a wash of misery, she watched the shape of his tall figure disappear around the bend of a cluster of trees—the broad shoulders, the shirt with its newly ironed creases put there by whomever did his laundry, the charming way he spoke with the ladies.

The other women continued to chatter around Willa, but she couldn't speak for a moment. Her pulse never subsided to normal till Harrison was well gone from view, and she was still staring at the deserted trees with the empty tin bowl in her fingers.

Sitting on the bench in the tavern gardens, six nights later, Willa inhaled a deep breath of fresh air and gazed up at the full moon. Sandwiched between the mountains that were shaded in hues of purple, the moon's face gazed down at her.

A twinge of loneliness ruffled her composure. She wondered what her youngest cousins, Adam and Derek, only three and four years older than her, were doing at this moment.

Voices behind her made her jump and turn.

Harrison was backing into the yard, oblivious of Willa as he closed the wooden gate behind him to keep out whomever he was talking to. "Perhaps you should call it a night, ladies. Your brothers will be worried where you are."

The women called over the gate, invisible to Willa save for their voices.

"My brother left for the gold fields last week."

"And my landlady doesn't mind my having visitors."

"Good night, ladies," he insisted.

"We'll wait for you inside," one purred.

Willa watched him sigh and rub his forehead. "All right."

He waited until he heard fading footsteps before he turned around. When he did, his wide shoulders dropped at seeing Willa.

Feeling awkward, she tugged at her shawl. "Shamus took over for a few minutes. Just needed to rest my feet. In fact, I should get up and—"

"Don't let me scare you away." He moved closer, shoving his hands into his pockets.

She nodded gently. "All right."

He slid onto the bench next to her. She didn't blame him, for they both spent so much time on their feet that sitting down any chance they could was a godsend.

He was so tall and muscled that there was very little room between them, and his shoulder brushed hers. He tried pulling his arm back but must've felt that made it look too obvious that he was trying to avoid her, so he allowed his arm to fall back where it was.

She bet he was sorry now, in their awkward silence, that he'd gotten trapped here with her. But the top of her shoulder warmed next to his.

"I've been meaning to apologize for six days," she said softly.

"Can't think of what for."

"Let's put it this way. In answer to your first question, I come from a small town named Scholar's Depot, thirty miles north of Billings."

He nodded. "Sounds like a smart place. Full of scholars."

"Nah. Maybe the folks who founded it were, but the rest of us are pretty daft."

He laughed at her joke and the tension in her neck faded.

"And as for your second question, my uncle and cousins—" she swallowed "—don't know I'm in Alaska."

"You tore off without telling them?"

She nodded, not proud of the fact, now that she had to say it aloud to Harrison.

He nodded as if it was a good thing. "I like spontaneity."

Her turn to smile.

"Well, I guess they got quite a jolt when they hollered for their breakfast and there was no one around to make it for them."

Shocked at his accurate summation, she twisted her shoulders to look up at him. "How did you know?"

"I guessed. You said you learned how to mix drinks by serving them. And that woman thing again. You know, put in your place. And why else would someone like you leave her family?"

Her eyes watered at the word *family*. Maybe she'd left too abruptly. Maybe she should have given them another chance. Or maybe, she thought, knowing that things for her never would've changed in Montana, she should've just accepted her lot there and made the most of it. Waited till they all got married—if they got married—and then opted for matrimony herself, perhaps to one of the older ranch hands her uncle was always suggesting.

"You might've guessed a whole slew of reasons for my leaving."

"Such as?"

Was this a game? She could play, she thought with a sense of adventure. "Maybe I came to find my fortune."

"If you mean gold, you didn't head to the gold fields."

"Maybe I came to find a man."

He struggled to bite down on his smile. "Haven't seen you say yes to anyone who's asked you to join him for dinner, or a stroll by the ocean."

Her face heated at the reminder of how she'd turned him down for the stroll.

"And there was the bit with the eager groom, remember?"

The playful antics stopped. The subject was getting serious again, but Harrison had no way of knowing it. She hadn't given him much information on why exactly she'd escaped Skagway, and just how bad a situation she'd been in. She wove her fingers together and studied them in her lap.

"What's his name, anyway? The idiot groom?"

"Keenan Crawford," she blurted this time without hesitation, feeling the gentle release of finally being able to tell someone. "Skagway's only butcher."

"Hmm," Harrison murmured. He let the moment slip by without probing.

It was comforting, the heat from his biceps seeping into her shoulder, him sitting and simply listening with no pressure.

"I feel safe here, Harrison. Working with you at the tavern."

Harrison's eyes flicked with tenderness. He reached out with one of those large tanned hands and clasped her fingers, letting his warm palm sit on top of hers on her lap. Just like that. Simply let his hand sit.

She didn't feel like moving.

She didn't feel like breathing.

She didn't feel like anything except staying here

with Harrison, staring up at the moon, listening to the insects buzzing and the calling of the loons.

"Hear the wolf?" Harrison whispered.

"No," she whispered back, then strained to listen. There it was. A very low howl somewhere deep in the mountains.

"My first Alaskan wolf."

He smiled at her, warm with pride, as if he'd pointed out something rare and beautiful.

She wanted him to kiss her.

Oh, yes, she did. She felt it in the tug of her abdomen, the weakness in her thighs, the throbbing of her pulse and the robbing of her breath.

Maybe he wanted to. It certainly looked like it by the angle of his head and the way his gaze dropped to her lips. When he leaned over, she closed her eyes in heated anticipation and heard nothing except the crazy thunder of her pulse in her head.

She felt his lips brush her forehead. Her *forehead*.

"See you inside."

Her eyes sprang open in humiliation that he'd likely known she was expecting a kiss on the mouth, only to witness him leaving again by the gate.

Crawford cursed at the list of problems he was forced to solve.

Sitting high atop his saddle on the best stallion this side of the Pacific, surrounded by four of his fiercest men as they congregated in a swath of darkness set against the moon and fading midnight sunshine, he listened to the details.

Dooley spit out a wad of tobacco. The movement shook his skinny frame, silhouetted against the sky. "Miller is griping again about the price of beef for his restaurant."

"Double the prices we charge him," Crawford snarled. "I hate complainers."

Dooley nodded coolly. "The fella who runs the gaming tables at the Nugget is stirring up a fuss. Doesn't like the late hours we keep at the butcher shop, unloading our wagons of beef outside his back doors."

"He lives in a fine house by the water. Burn it down. He'll scramble to rebuild before the snow hits, and that'll keep him occupied and out of our hair for the next two months."

"That fella Clive we told you about last week still won't cooperate. Doesn't want to sell us any more horses."

"Slit his throat," Crawford ordered.

The sound of hooves galloping closer hushed the men. Crawford peered into the darkness till the skinny shape of Tyrone, on horseback, became clearer.

"There's word," Tyrone shouted, his long blond hair fluttering in the wind. "Word about the girl."

Crawford leaned over his saddle horn, eager to hear it.

Breathless, Tyrone eased his mare next to Crawford's mount. Crawford's stallion whinnied and reared, smelling the mare. Crawford grinned at the animal attraction and reined his beast to submission.

"What is it?" he snapped, irritated that the man took so long to speak.

Tyrone fought to suck in air. "Miss Somerset was spotted the night she disappeared."

Chapter Seven

Two days later, still recovering from the kiss that never happened that night in the gardens, Willa was working the lunch hour when two ladies stepped into the brightly lit tavern and joined Harrison at one of the back tables. Willa groaned when she saw them coming. It wasn't easy serving Harrison's female guests, especially in front of the man himself.

There was a scattering of noon customers in the place, not nearly as crowded as the evenings, so Willa was left to serve the drinks on her own while sending the lunch orders on to the kitchen.

Balancing a heavy tray above her shoulders, Willa squeezed through the chairs and slid two glasses of ale to a fisherman and his crewmate at the sunny table by the window.

The bearded man nodded. "Thank you, miss."

"Your sandwiches will be right along."

Harrison flagged her. She trudged to the back wall, her skirts swishing about the planks. "Yes, sir?"

"Some ladies here who'd like a bite to eat."

Willa tried not to seem impatient, but she had better things to do than entertain these characters. She'd met them before, and quite frankly, they were rude. Willa knew darn well by the way one was batting her lashes at Harrison, and the way the other was leaning so close that her cleavage was spilling out the top of her blouse, that these two ladies weren't here for the canned beef.

Turning away and ignoring her as they were made Willa squirm with discomfort. She wasn't sure exactly why, but figured it was because they always made her feel very unfeminine.

Harrison was in a white shirt and tan suede vest, working on his business journals and records at the other side of the table. The ladies had helped themselves to sitting at his table. He whisked a large hand through the dark hair at his temples and studied a column of numbers.

Determined to be cheery, Willa smiled at the brunette with perfumed hair and took out her pad of paper. "Priscilla? What can I get you?"

"Nothing too filling. I am watching my figure." Priscilla's eyes twitched over Willa's waistline. "Some of us have to. Honestly, Willa, I don't see how you can work as a bartender. It's a man's duty. I prefer to stay firmly on the side of femininity. Which includes watching what I eat."

"Ah," said Willa. "Then you won't be ordering the large fisherman's platter like you did last week, with two servings of pudding?"

Priscilla's forehead turned pink. She turned to Harrison, but he was frowning over a column and hadn't appeared to have heard. "Apple cider. *Please.* With a scone and sliced cheese."

Willa turned to the other young lady and braced herself for more. "Lidia?"

Lidia fanned her face with her floppy hat. "Grilled salmon and a lemonade. And I do agree with Priscilla. Why on earth you'd prefer to pour drinks all day than work in some pretty little place pinning dresses together, I'll never understand. But then I suppose, Harrison, you probably don't even notice her gender anymore?"

Harrison looked up at the call of his name.

Willa's nostrils flared. Her mouth flew open as she sputtered for a quick retort, about to tell the young woman exactly what she could do with her salmon when Harrison answered.

"Choosing a profession is an individual decision. Miss Banks is excellent at hers."

The two ladies puckered their mouths as if they were tasting something sour.

Willa glanced down at her paper and tried to hide a smile of satisfaction. Harrison's protective side was showing, and she was flattered. However, since he was the most eligible bachelor in town, and these ladies were obviously here to see if they could remedy that, it was best Willa be left out of the equation.

"She's better than most men I could've hired," Harrison added. "Although...I definitely notice..." He trailed off. The lines of his dark cheeks tightened.

The table grew silent and Willa felt her skin flush.

If Harrison stood up for her, Willa would never live down the gossip. The innuendos that perhaps they were more than boss and bartender. She had to defend herself, not have him speaking up too loudly on her behalf. Not if she wanted to avoid tongues from wagging.

Willa drew herself together and kept her tone light. "So that was grilled salmon, lemonade, a scone and apple cider. May I get you anything else?"

"That's all," said Priscilla. "Run along now. There are kegs to be hauled and drinks to be stirred." She snorted in laughter.

Lidia giggled.

Willa's mouth prickled with humiliation.

Harrison's face turned grim.

Oh, no.

The two seated women looked at him and snapped to attention, but it was too late to placate him.

Rising to full height, he motioned them toward the door. Willa had never heard the rough tone of his voice before. "I would appreciate it if you would both leave. Please come back when you've found your manners. You'll have to excuse me now. I have kegs to haul and drinks to stir."

On the inside—the side she couldn't show anyone, not even him—Willa silently cheered. Her pulse soared at his words and his chivalrous defense. But on the outside she lowered her eyes so as not to cause too much embarrassment to the women, turned and got back to the duties she'd been hired for.

Harrison really did appreciate her. This man truly did value her hard work and contributions.

The warm sun streamed over Harrison's shoulder the next morning as the mustang beneath him strained forward, galloping hard and fast across the grasslands. It was a well-worn path, one in which he'd lately been seeking solace more and more frequently to clear his mind.

He enjoyed the blast of the wind on his face. His shoulders heaved beneath the blazing sun, and he inhaled air as fresh as the ice cap on the mountains next to him.

The ocean was on his other side, waves cresting and rolling as far as the eye could see. Alaskan freedom never felt so dear and strong as when he was high atop his horse.

He'd been dreaming again of Elizabeth. She'd

come to him, slender and shapely in the middle of the night, gently kissing his ear and telling him she was going for a ride that morning. Just as she had the day she'd died.

Except in his dream, he knew the danger looming. Tried to warn her that the coming storm was dangerous, that the horses in the corral were spooked by the thunder and lightning, that they'd break out of the gates and trample her in the mud.

But none of those words of warning had left his lips. Not in his dream, nor in life.

"Don't worry so much," she'd told him in the dream, kissing him lightly on the shoulder and disappearing out the door. *"Don't worry so much."*

He jumped right after her through the doorway, but she was gone. The hallway empty. It was impossible to disappear so quickly. Physics wouldn't allow it.

He'd shouted and shouted, "Elizabeth! Elizabeth!" But no one appeared.

With his heart pounding in a frenzy, he'd jumped with a start from his bed, then realized it was another one of his nightmares.

So he'd shoved on his jeans, tore down the stairs, through the empty kitchen and found himself on his mare.

If he couldn't get that scene with Elizabeth out of his mind while sleeping, maybe he could push it out of his head at the exhilarating speed of thirty miles an hour.

The wind rushed his ears. The horse's mane flew past his hands. The sound of steady hooves smacked the hardened ground while his breath panted in and out.

Maybe he'd die just like Elizabeth. That's what he wanted, wasn't it? To disappear and never feel that empty hollow pit in his chest again?

As fast and agile as the mustang was on her feet, and knowing that this breed always kept some energy in reserve, Harrison let her run for ten more minutes before tugging gently on the reins to slow her to a trot. He leaned over and gave her a pat.

"Good girl. You did good."

No, dying wasn't what he wanted.

But since the arrival of Willa, the nightmares of Elizabeth had returned.

Making a right at the end of the path just before the gully, Harrison turned toward the few cabins that outlined the outskirts of Eagle's Cliff and headed for his livery stables in the clearing.

He nodded to a few townsfolk walking on the boardwalk—the postal clerk, a shopkeeper, the tinsmith. When Harrison entered his corral, the stable hand was watering and exercising two quarter horses that one of the hotel guests had checked in with last night.

"Morning, Billy." Harrison eyed the red-haired young man who was always quick with a smile.

"Boss. Take a gander at these fine animals. Pure

muscle. I reckon they could pull a house, if I chained it right behind them."

Harrison nodded with agreement. "See if the owner needs anything in terms of supply. Tell him we've got a vet lives just a mile away, if he needs any care."

"Sure, boss."

Harrison slid off his mount. Taking his mare by the reins, he headed into the stables to put her back into her stall.

On his way through the door, he heard Willa's voice. "Chuck, you must realize how smart donkeys are."

The comment caught Harrison off guard. It was an unusual thing to say, and the troubles on his mind faded as his curiosity grew.

She was stroking the gray donkey belonging to another guest, hand-feeding it oats. With a loose, cream-colored blouse, long brown skirt and her blond hair tied back with a simple ribbon, she looked fresh and energetic. As though she'd had no trouble sleeping.

Chuck, in a checkered shirt and dungarees, with pitchfork in hand, was busy spreading fresh straw in the animal's stall.

"Donkeys are far more intelligent than horses," she said, "but most folks don't realize it. Isn't that right, Rufus?" she asked the donkey. "We had one on the ranch that could answer questions."

Harrison tried to stifle a grin but couldn't. "Could he tell you how much two and two added up to?"

She wheeled around with a look of surprise when she saw him, and he added as he walked by, "Let me guess. He stomped his hoof four times?"

"No," she corrected him. "No matter how far away from home he was, we'd ask him what direction home was, and he'd point his nose. He was always right."

"Impressive." Harrison led his mustang to the far stall.

"Better than some people."

"What else could he do?" Harrison called.

She fed the donkey a carrot. "If you asked him to find water, he would. Sometimes he'd lead you to the river. Sometimes he'd find a puddle."

"Could he speak French?"

She laughed. "When my cousin Adam was small, if you asked *him* how much two and two was, he'd stomp *his* foot."

Now she was kidding Harrison and he laughed, too. "You like your cousin Adam."

Her lashes flickered. Her smile turned wistful. "Yeah. I did."

She spoke in the past tense, as if she'd decided she was never going to see him again.

Didn't she want to set things right? Was there really no point in returning to her home in Montana? Ever?

"Scholar's Depot," said Harrison. "Maybe the name applies to the animals more than the people."

That brought out her smile again. "The animals are brilliant."

He settled his mustang and filled the water trough. Willa continued feeding Rufus, Chuck moved to another stall and all that could be heard was the munching of animals and the occasional shuffling of a boot.

The scent of the straw around him and the warmth inside the stables made Harrison stretch the time. He really should be going into the tavern to spell out the duties of the cooks today. He should check on the guests and see to it that the housekeeping maid made up room number five for double occupancy tonight.

Yet, he waited and passed the time here in the stables with Willa nearby. It had been an odd conversation, one of a light topic, yet he felt as though the weight of his troubles had been lifted if only for these few moments before breakfast.

He'd been thinking too much of Elizabeth lately and didn't know how to stop it.

"Aren't you going to bed?" George scraped off the grill as he spoke to Harrison at one-thirty that night.

Natalie hung the newly washed pots above the stove, also trying to tidy up quickly so she and George could get home to bed.

Harrison shrugged. "Just a few more things to do." He brought in logs from the garden, where he'd split them earlier and stacked them beside the fireplace.

"That can wait till morning," George told him. "It's firewood, for Pete's sake."

Natalie gave her husband a stern look of warning, as if telling him not to agitate the boss.

"He's takin' to working crazy hours," George explained to his wife. "Long after we're gone, he's still up for God knows how long." He turned back to Harrison. "It's not my place, but you feel like a son to me, and I'm tellin' you, you need some sleep. Willa's already gone. Shamus locked up and disappeared half an hour ago. We're leaving, too, and you're starting another chore."

Because he didn't want to sleep. Didn't want to dream.

Harrison straightened up and nodded at Natalie. "Don't get mad at him, Natalie. He's just speaking his mind. I take your point, George. Good night, the both of you."

"'Night, Harrison," she said as she took her shawl and disappeared with her husband out the back door. They only lived half a block down the street, so it wasn't far to go.

Harrison tossed the log to the fireplace and locked up behind them.

He washed up in the spring room. It had a fireplace, porcelain tub and a personal cupboard filled with his extra clothes. It was too late to heat water for a bath, so he scrubbed his face and brushed his teeth before toweling off and climbing the stairs to bed.

It seemed he'd no sooner gotten to sleep than Elizabeth came calling to him again.

"Don't worry so much," she told him.

He was just running into the hallway, searching for her, the silent screams tearing through his body when he heard a gunshot.

Even in his dream, he thought the occurrence odd. There'd been no guns involved in her death. Just the hooves of six twelve-hundred-pound animals. Twenty-four hooves. They bore down on him now, as he tried to get up from the mud. They were coming…he could hear the panting of the beasts…the rumbling of hooves echoing through the mud that held him stuck, sprawled out in the sticky paste… then an odd voice came calling.

"Harrison? You in there?"

A man's voice. Who was that? How did the voice fit into Harrison's nightmare?

Knuckles rapped on his door.

He jolted out of bed.

"Harrison," called Billy through the door as Harrison rubbed an eye and tried to get his bearings.

Was it morning already?

Light beamed gently through the curtains, but the

golden rays seemed dimmer than six o'clock, his usual waking time.

"Come quick." Billy pounded on the door but not as hard as he could, perhaps not to wake anyone else. Panic mounted in his words. "Someone got to the livestock. They stole the animals. They shot Chuck!"

Chapter Eight

Willa bolted out of bed at the commotion in the hall and peered at her pocket watch on the night stand. It read three o'clock. What was going on? She hurried to dress—with no time to lace into a corset. She threw on her chemise, pantaloons, skirt and blouse and rushed out to see Harrison leaping down the stairs behind his stable hand, Billy.

"That's why I heard the gunshot in my dream," Harrison was telling Billy. "It wasn't in my dream. It was coming from the stables."

"What is it?" she cried after them.

Harrison turned his wide shoulder toward her but kept walking. "Horse thieves!"

She gasped and struggled to comprehend the implications. Room doors opened around her. Two gold miners poked their heads out, as did a young carpenter from down the hall.

She flew down the stairs after Harrison, squeezing through the aisles of the kitchen and the hanging pots. Her stomach tightened as she noted that both men wore holsters and guns. "Is anyone hurt?"

Harrison shoved the back door and strode out through the dimly lit gardens, heading for the stables. The sun was hiding behind the mountains, its low rays gilding the trees and shrubs.

"One man down," Harrison told her.

Her boots tore through the soil as she shoved the tail end of her blouse into her skirt. "Who?"

Billy adjusted his cowboy hat over his head of long red hair as Harrison stepped into the corral. "Chuck."

Her heart tripped. Chuck was not much older than she was. A kind young man who'd been trained with horses and guns on a spread in New Mexico. A lump wedged in her throat. Not dead, she prayed, please not dead.

He was hurt pretty badly, judging by the blood on the straw around him as Willa approached the stall he was lying in. She could barely look. Three men held him down as a white-haired gent with a medicine bag rushed in—the doctor she'd heard had a practice in town, whom she'd never met. Dr. Lawrence Leighton.

He eased down on the red straw and examined the seeping thigh that someone had already tied a shirt around, as a tourniquet to quell the bleeding.

"Chuck." Harrison eased himself onto the other side of the straw, and Willa's throat tightened with the soothing comfort in his voice. "Easy with your breathing. Take a deep breath and let it out slow."

"Broken leg," the doctor said to Harrison. "Lost a lot of blood. Artery's nicked but not severed. Bullet went right through, so at least I won't have to dig it out."

With gnarled, agile hands, the doctor cleaned the wound with tonic and wrapped fresh bandaging above and below the break in the leg. The doctor's long white hair billowed over his ears and fell like frostbitten grass over his thinning scalp. He strained to tie the last knot. "There. Bleeding's stopped."

Chuck closed his eyes, fading into unconsciousness, then snapped them open again. His face was the palest Willa had ever seen on a man, something akin to a sheet of paper. The pain had to be horrendous.

Chuck groaned, sputtered, then heaved forward and vomited. Harrison quickly rolled Chuck toward himself so that Chuck was in a side-lying position, and talked to the injured man in calming tones.

"Take it easy. You're going to be all right. Doc's going to give you something for the pain."

Chuck vomited again, hitting Harrison's pants with the spray, but Harrison didn't budge out of position. Willa was struck by the kindness in Harrison's reaction. He had a commanding presence in the company of his men. And her.

"Is there a clean blanket around here anyplace?" He looked up and met her eyes. There was a jolt of intensity between them.

Yes, something she could do to help. She raced to the office in the corner, picked out six newly laundered towels and the freshest-smelling wool blanket there was—likely used to wash down the animals. She rushed to bring it back, bending over Chuck in the stall, not caring that she was kneeling in the messy straw herself.

Harrison tucked the blanket around Chuck's upper half to keep him warm and calm. He took a towel and wiped Chuck's face.

The vomiting stopped. The doctor drew up a syringe of clear medicine, tugged at Chuck's sleeve and injected the concoction into his bicep.

It was then she noticed the silence.

As they waited for the painkiller to take effect, the neighbors who'd come running at the commotion— two who still wore the long johns they'd been sleeping in—plus Billy, Harrison, the doctor and Chuck, were as still as a sea without wind, not a ripple among them.

The stables were empty. No large animals left. The donkey, Rufus, was gone. Harrison's mustang in the far corner, too. Plus the two quarter horses, and whatever other animals she didn't know about. Sadness crept through her. What had happened to the gentle beasts?

"Take the lady out of here, please," said the doc.

She frowned. "But I'm an extra pair of hands. I'll do whatever you say."

"Then come back in five minutes. We've got some bone resettin' to do."

She gulped, jumped to her feet and flew out. She stepped outside to the corral, inhaling a deep breath of fresh early morning air, looking toward the serenity of the mountains with their forested slopes and milk-coated tops.

Seconds later, Chuck's screams screeched up her spine. Lord, have mercy. Her body shook. But she knew—just knew in her soul—that Harrison, with his God-given strength, and the doctor were doing everything possible.

When the screams died down, so did her shakes. She turned around and raced back inside. Maybe there was something more—anything—she could do to ease the situation for her friends.

It was an hour later when things started to calm down and Harrison could get some straight answers. Chuck had been moved to the doctor's house for rest and twenty-four-hour care. The old man had a housekeeper who came in and helped during the day, a woman he was training as a nurse.

Three neighbors who'd rushed into the stable to help were loading the soiled straw to a wheelbarrow, where they'd take it outdoors and burn it.

"How many thieves were there?" Harrison looked at the faces as they heaved their pitchforks. Behind them, Willa was folding the clean towels that'd been left behind by the doctor.

"At least three," said Billy. "They were real quiet. We couldn't hear them in the bunkhouse. But Chuck said he caught the rustle of hooves, so he got up to investigate. Before I could get my pants on, I heard the gunshot."

"I heard it, too." Harrison rubbed his neck. "Wish I…" He didn't finish the sentence, but the sentiment of regret filled his voice. If only he'd woken up at the sound. He might've caught the would-be murderers and saved the animals.

Hellfire.

"What'd they look like?"

"Two scrawny blond ones in their twenties, maybe. A heavier, dark-set gunslinger in his thirties."

"What direction did they head?"

"The mountains," said Billy.

"The water," said another fellow.

Harrison winced. Opposite directions.

"I thought there were only two men," said the tinsmith. "Both dark and heavy."

Conflicting reports didn't help, either.

"It's the gang we've been hearing about," said Harrison. "They knew exactly how to enter and leave without being seen. Anyone spot any strangers here in the past few days?"

Some of the men shrugged. Billy rubbed his forehead.

"I have." Willa stepped forward, her hair askew, but looking soft and comforting, nonetheless, to Harrison. "I serve strangers every night."

The tinsmith raised his eyebrows. "No disrespect, miss, but you're new in town and everyone's a stranger to you here."

"That's not entirely true," she said. "I do know some faces. Some have become regulars. It's true I don't know as many as the rest of you, but there were two scrawny men with blond hair who sat at the far table two nights ago, nursing their drinks for about four hours."

"Why's that unusual? That's what men come to do."

"They weren't paying me any attention, that's what. Not that every man I walk past has to look my way…" She swallowed and slid her gaze at the circle of faces, sliding her hand down her skirt as if suddenly self-conscious of what she was saying.

"Go on," said Harrison. "I'd like to hear your point."

"It's just that most men pay me some attention, that's all. And yet those two men, related in some way, I could see it in their faces, those two customers never looked my way."

"Maybe they had other things on their mind," the tinsmith insisted.

"But," she said, "when they thought I wasn't looking, whenever I turned my back at the bar, that's when they would stare at me and follow my movements."

"If your back was turned, how do you know?"

"I watched them in the wall mirror."

Harrison's hopes lifted. "Keep going."

"They weren't staring at me, as a woman, so I didn't think they were after *me*," she said with emphasis to Harrison, meaning she didn't suspect Crawford had sent them. "They were watching Shamus, too. I could see they were interested in what we were doing. Opening the till, registering the hotel guests, bringing up the luggage. There's been so much interest in your tavern, Harrison, that I chalked it up to harmless curiosity and didn't mention it. But looking back, I suspect they were casing the place for what they could steal."

"Did you overhear anything?"

"Every time I got close they stopped talking."

Harrison's hopes fell again.

"But they had soiled boots. Muddy. There were dried patches on their pant legs, white stains that went up to their knees."

"Salt water," said Harrison. "They came by the ocean."

She nodded. He was impressed by her attention to detail, and her stoic ability to have stood by for the last little while to help deal with Chuck and his injuries.

"Anything else?"

"Not that I can think of."

"Go get Shamus," Harrison told one of the men. "You know where he lives." Too far away from the stables, obviously, to have heard the gunshot and commotion to come running. "Maybe he noticed the two men in the bar that night, too."

One of the fishermen lifted his pitchfork and stabbed at clean straw to spread it around the stall.

"I'd be mighty appreciative," said Harrison, "if one of you men would take a boat to Skagway and notify my brother, Quinn, that I need him up here. And notify the deputy marshal of the problem we're having."

A volunteer quickly stepped forward—a fisherman who had his own boat, a young likeable fellow by the name of Zeb Abrams. "I'll go. Want me to leave now?"

"Yeah. Take a note with you." Harrison went into his office, scratched out a few sentences, tucked the paper into an envelope, sealed it with wax and returned it to Zeb. "Thank you all for your help."

Heads nodded around the group.

"Let us know if you need anything more," one of them called as they exited for their various duties.

Billy looked down at Harrison's pants and boots, splattered with blood and vomit. "You need to clean up, boss."

Harrison looked down. He'd forgotten what a

mess he was. There was nothing else to do at this moment except return to the tavern, clean up and be available to reassure guests and staff as they arrived for the day.

Where was Willa? He scoured the stables. No sign of blond hair. No curvy figure. He wanted to thank her, too, and tell her how much it meant to him that she'd stayed to help.

There she was—heading out the front door. She turned around unexpectedly, her hair a tangle of light and dark, eyes as soft as misty dew. She held up a hand toward him in a simple wave goodbye, and Harrison noted, for the first time since rising, that the buttons on her blouse were done up wrong. She'd missed the top buttonhole and started too far down. Her blouse ruffled over her bosom and she seemed completely unaware the fabric puckered up on one side, that the lacy collar fell across the soft hollow of her throat at a slant. The whole picture only added to her charm.

Stay, he longed to tell her. Instead, he planted his palm in the air in a similar gesture to hers and mouthed the words, "Thank you."

She turned and walked out.

Beside him, Billy ran a hand through his red hair and sighed. Harrison was brought back to the situation at hand. He was reminded how hard it must be for the young man. Billy and Chuck had become inseparable these past few weeks.

Harrison peered at him. "You up for tracking these men?"

Billy's shoulders straightened. "Yes, sir."

"I'd like you to ask Zeb's brother, Michael, to join you. He's a good tracker and a careful shot, from what I've heard. I'll pay you both."

Shamus ran in then, out of breath with his shirt hanging out of his denim jeans. "I just heard!"

Harrison expanded on the news and peppered him with questions as Shamus tried to fathom Chuck's injuries. "Will he be all right?"

Billy interjected. "Doc Leighton says he's seen worse breaks and the men survived."

"That's what we have to hope for." Harrison nodded to Billy. "Get ready to leave. The tinsmith said he'd lend us horses."

"I'll get Michael. We'll come back here to study the tracks before we go. Should be daylight by then." Billy grabbed his cowboy hat off the boards and headed toward the bunkhouse to clean up and pack.

Harrison turned to Shamus. "Did you notice the two scrawny men in the bar that Willa described?"

Shamus rubbed his forehead. "We see so many people…I don't believe so."

Harrison tried not to show his disappointment. "Can you go inside the hotel and calm down any guests?"

"Yes, sir." Shamus slapped his hat on his thigh and left.

Harrison hadn't allowed his anger to overtake him in front of the others, but it spilled out now. It made his stomach quake. Yet, calmly, he studied the stall where Chuck had fallen. Two cows, two quarter horses, the mustang and the donkey were missing. Was it just a random theft?

Fury coiled in his chest, ready to spring at the men responsible. He made his way through the dimly lit gardens toward the tavern. He guessed it to be shortly after four. When he was close to the back door, Shamus came out.

"Everyone's asleep," said Shamus. "Willa said she reassured a couple of people and they went back to their rooms. The owners of the stolen livestock are still sleeping. Should I wake them?"

"It's my responsibility. I'll tell them the bad news as soon as I clean up."

"I'll go help Billy at the bunkhouse. See if he needs anything more."

"Much obliged."

Harrison slid into the back door of the kitchen. All was still and silent. He craned his ear to the stairway. No creaking of wood risers. Willa had gone back to bed, too, he surmised.

He was alone.

He looked down at his bloodied clothes. He'd never get clean unless he took a quick bath. As he passed the fireplace, he reached for the empty cauldron that he would fill with water and heat up in the spring room. He stored a cupboard in there with clean work clothes. The spring room was where the housekeeper ironed his shirts and folded his jeans.

Unbuttoning his stained shirt, he made his way down the darkened hall. Inches away from the closed door, Harrison set the empty cauldron on the floor and slid out of his dirty shirt. The cool rustle of morning air greeted his bare skin. He'd have to get out of his stained pants and boots, too, so he tore out of those and put the clothing in the hamper at the far corner, where the housekeeper would see them.

Stripped down to his drawers, he picked up the cauldron again and turned the doorknob. The door was stiff to move, so he gave it a shove and stepped inside the hot, steamy room.

He wasn't alone, after all.

He froze, his pulse spinning when Willa turned around near the blazing fireplace. She gasped in equal surprise, wearing only a cotton chemise as she toweled off her beautiful bare legs.

Chapter Nine

Willa could barely breathe at Harrison's arrival.

The empty cauldron slid from his fingers, indicating his surprise, and thudded against the wooden floor.

She realized she likely hadn't heard the doorknob open because of the crackling fire logs.

Harrison gave a quick glance back at the door latch, which he'd uprooted and had quietly tore right out of the pine. He turned back to her, naked except for his short drawers, aghast with apology. The still of the night emphasized the impropriety of being nearly naked herself, how alone they were and how volatile the situation.

Heat seeped up her chest and neck and lingered in her cheeks. Her mouth went dry. Her arms felt heavy as she crossed them over her breasts.

Outside, through the window, the midnight sun

still hovered behind the mountains. It cast warm orange light over the furnishings indoors—the soft rag rug that squished between her bare toes, the fire that gently sputtered beside her, warming her bare thighs, and the loose chemise that had been the quickest thing to pull on earlier, but was see-through to her nipples.

Her gaze flashed over him. Dear Lord, his bare chest was riddled with scars. The most prominent, the freshest injury, was on the left side of his lower ribs, a red blotch of tissue the size of three knuckles.

She wondered if he still encountered pain. She didn't think so, since his movements were always graceful and fluid in the stables. And she'd never noticed any stiffness when she worked alongside him in the tavern.

By the door where he stood, basins of heated water were lined up in ceramic jugs. A bathtub with bronzed claw feet stood in the center of the room, slightly offside, although empty because she'd decided to wash standing up.

Neither said a word as they sized each other up, perhaps not wanting to scare the other into bolting.

Why, she wondered, was she so riveted by this man?

Riveted by those dark eyes that moved from her face, traveled down her breasts, over her skivvies and down the length of her legs.

She appraised him, too. The width of his tanned

chest, the muscles that flexed around his breastbone, the artery that throbbed in his neck as he watched her, the lean stomach and flat muscles that trailed into the tops of his drawers. He'd shed his pants outside somewhere, leaving the dirt behind, obviously fully intending to wash up in what he'd assumed would be the privacy of the spring room.

Say something, she thought.

Say something to let me know what you're thinking and why you should go. Tell me you're sorry for disturbing me, that you weren't aware I was in here alone.

Tell me anything. But don't just stand there making me agonize about the next decision. Forcing me to be the one to ask you to leave.

Tell me, tell me, tell me.

He swallowed, his Adam's apple moving up and down, the slight shadow of a beard prickling through his skin.

He took a step closer, reached for a sponge between the water jugs, dipped it in, stepped in front of her and with all the boldness of a lion tamer, squeezed the sponge onto her bare shoulder.

The water trickled down her muscle to her underarm, a blast of warmth in the cool morning air.

Standing inches away, looking down into her eyes as if challenging her to question what he was doing, he took the sponge and squeezed it over her other shoulder.

The water drizzled in rivulets along her skin, down her arms and the side of her breasts. Heat seeped into the soft cotton fabric of her undershirt, making its way to her nipples. The delicious liquid sensation made her nipples tighten.

As he looked down at the outline of her pink nipples against the sheer cloth, his pupils flickered.

A tightness wove its way into her belly, a tremulous shudder of expectation and a fear of what they were doing.

What *he* was doing, soaking her skin and inviting himself to bathe her.

Yet, she stood unmoving, breathless and incapable of arguing.

She wanted this to happen. The silent caress of his eyes, the eager twist of his mouth, the concentration on his brow. This was a man who'd demonstrated such gentleness an hour earlier when he'd taken care of a wounded stable hand, who'd surprised her with his ease and effortless command of the situation.

And now, it seemed, he was under her spell.

Whatever she had that was drawing him held him frozen to the spot, barefooted in short drawers on the rag rug before her, standing in full height in all his glory.

In a flash, she flicked her lashes lower down his chest and saw that an erection strained against the linen of his drawers.

With the shock of that sight, an indication of where this was leading, the fear that she'd be forced, she took a step backward and shook her head.

Harrison couldn't get enough of looking at her. With her back to the glowing fire, she was as beautiful a woman as he'd ever seen. He could well understand how, over the ages, men had painted and sculpted and even killed for the remarkably beautiful female form.

The tips of her breasts were soaked clear through the sheer cotton gauze. Rounded areolae formed a pink shadow around raised nipples, making his mouth water and his blood pound. The cotton fabric was dry around the flat wall of her stomach and, although she had a towel covering the apex of her naked thighs, her gorgeous legs were an invitation in themselves.

She wasn't wearing petticoats or pantaloons. Smooth skin, a mile long, stretched from her hips to her slender knees, down her calves and to the tips of pretty toes.

But this was too much. Too much for him.

Without another word, he dropped the sponge, took a few steps to the chest of drawers beneath the window, pulled out a clean pair of jeans, shirt and underclothes.

He also grabbed a clean towel. Without looking back to Willa, he opened the door and called over his shoulder. "I'll wash up at the stables. There's no one there."

When he closed the door, he took a moment to collect himself, sagging against the cool plank wall and closing his eyes.

He didn't even know her true name.

Who she really was and where she planned on going. He had no business getting involved with her when she'd come here to escape another man.

He had no business sponging her shoulder or arm or any other damn part of her body, when the only thought pounding through his brain was how much he wanted to feel her naked, pressed beneath him.

He'd had his share of paid women when Elizabeth had passed. Several years filled with cheap nights, perfumed tricks and a feeling of shallowness the following morning when he'd woken up and discovered the insufferable loneliness was still there, no matter how frenzied the sex had been the night before.

It was the loneliness he couldn't stand.

It was ten times stronger *after* having a fling and discovering they meant nothing to each other, than it was the night before when the evening had started out flirtatious and filled with promise.

He could never bed Willa.

He could never take the chance that what he'd be giving up, another notch of his heart, might be the last notch he had.

Pulling on his jeans, he strode down the empty hall, out the empty kitchen and into the empty morning.

After breakfast, and regaining some composure after his encounter with Willa, Harrison tried to calm the half a dozen hotel guests as they stood outside the stables.

Shamus shuffled beside him, tall and bulky, his dark hair slicked back. The sun had risen and crested the mountaintops, as swollen as a plump orange, beating down on the back of Harrison's neck. He pushed back his Stetson to shade his skin.

Harrison listed the stolen items. "Three horses, one of which was my mustang, the other two belonging to Mr. Creemore, who left on a ship two days ago for a weeklong business trip. Two dairy cows. One donkey. The goats were left behind in a separate shack, as well as two rabbits."

"If I would've known how bad your security was, I never would've stayed here," an old miner scoffed.

"Mr. Beatty," Harrison replied, "you didn't even board any animals. I'm not sure what you're doing here."

"I'm a payin' customer, ain't I? I bet Creemore's gonna have your hide when he gets back!"

Harrison decided not to reply. He expected anger, he told himself. It would blow over.

He turned to the heavyset man on his right with

the muttonchop whiskers. "Mr. Mieler, I understand how upset you are, but please be more specific. Did the Holsteins have any recognizable features? Were they branded?"

The rotund man muttered in a German dialect. "One of the heifers has a piece missing off her left ear. She strayed into some barbwire. The other one has a big patch of white on her right side in the shape of a hand. But no brand."

Harrison's mustang hadn't been branded, either, so he knew the frustration. Branded livestock wasn't always necessary, if the animals weren't intended for the open range, where they were liable to stray.

"We'll do our best to catch them," Shamus told the man.

The couple who lost their donkey were the most upset. Newly married in their thirties, the Vanderbilts had lived a harsh life in California and had barely scraped together enough coins to get here. The donkey was their only asset.

With her hair pulled back starkly into a bun, the thin bride sniffled into a hanky. "Rufus is a gentle creature. His heart can't take too much excitement."

"How old is he?" Harrison peered down at them.

"Twenty-four years," her thin husband replied. "He's all we could afford."

"I'm surprised he survived the voyage here!"

Beatty piped up from behind the shoulders of the German man.

The comment made the bride burst into a fresh set of tears.

Harrison scowled at Beatty. "Now would be a good time to go get yourself some coffee."

"I'm not hankerin' for any," the man whined. But when the others also stared him down, he muttered something and slinked away. "I'm gonna tell Creemore all about this. He's a businessman. Won't take no excuses from anyone."

Beatty might've been the most vocal complainer here, but looking into the glistening, troubled eyes of the rest of the crowd, Harrison realized they were all upset.

He was responsible for the care of their animals. He pulled out a wad of bills, unfolded several and handed two twenties to the young couple. They hesitated, but the husband must've realized he was in no position to turn it down, so slid it from Harrison's fingers and nodded his thanks.

Shamus recorded the date and amount on his sheet of paper.

"Ain't near enough!" Beatty hollered from twenty paces away as he continued to the tavern. "For sure he didn't pay Alaska prices!"

Shamus muttered under his breath. Harrison nudged his assistant, indicating it was best to ignore the outburst.

Harrison turned to Mieler and handed him twice what he'd given the married couple. "Consider this partial payment if we don't recover your cows. If you'd like full payment, or want to sign ownership over to me, speak up now."

Mieler rubbed his whiskers. "Those two dairy cows produce more milk than any others I've ever had. I'll give you some time to bring 'em back."

"Thank you."

"We can give you a bit of time, too," said Mr. Vanderbilt. "But we were planning to head out into gold territory, day after tomorrow. Rufus was supposed to help us carry our things. We were countin' on him."

"We could try to locate another donkey," Harrison replied. "Or horse. I'd be happy to replace your animal."

The woman sobbed into her hanky again. "I'd like to wait for Rufus."

Harrison felt guilty as hell. "You can stay on at the tavern free of charge till we find him."

"Much obliged."

There wasn't more to say. Harrison had already explained how he was sending for help from the deputy marshal in Skagway, notifying his brother the district attorney, and how he'd sent two men out to track the thieves.

The crowd dispersed to the tavern.

Shamus took off his hat and slid it down his

side, resting past his holster. "Is it all right if I go say hello to Chuck?"

"Please do. Keep me notified."

"I checked on the rabbits. They're fine. And I let the goats out to pasture."

Harrison nodded and Shamus left.

He rubbed his hand over his newly shaven face. The scent of soap from his earlier wash-up in the stables drifted past his skin.

Harrison hadn't seen Willa since accidentally barging in on her in the spring room, and he wondered if she was sleeping. She deserved some rest. She deserved some time away from him.

He pulled down on the brim of his hat and spun toward his stables, intending to look things over more thoroughly in case he missed anything earlier, just in time to see Willa walking in off the boardwalk, twenty yards away.

His gut slammed.

Why on earth did he have such a strong reaction to her presence? What was it about this woman that made him physically aware of how she moved and how she looked?

She didn't notice him at first, as he made his way beneath the trees to the stables.

Hurrying down the cedar steps to the gardens, she lifted her skirts, revealing the white lace of her petticoats. By the constraint beneath her blouse, he surmised she'd taken the time to put on a corset.

Why was he doing this to himself? This torture of gauging her every movement, of looking at every inch of her body for clues of what lies beneath?

Just then, Willa looked up, turned her head and peered straight into his eyes. His breathing tripled and everything else flew out of his head.

Chapter Ten

Willa had to walk past Harrison on the pathway to make it to the kitchen, but her steps faltered. She was returning from a visit with Chuck at the doctor's, ensuring he had everything he needed, but Chuck had been asleep, finally resting comfortably.

Ten feet away, Harrison riveted her gaze.

With the sun behind his shoulders, he was a statue of a man. A solid block of muscled sinew and strength. To think, only a few hours previously, he'd seen her exposed in a manner that brought a rush of guilt to her heart and caused her skin to tingle with apprehension.

She should never have been so exposed to a man who wasn't her husband. Who didn't care for and love her, who didn't put her sensitivities first. A man who wasn't so bold that he just reached out and dripped water all over and made her feel…made her feel so…so feminine and natural, and blazes, so desirable she could barely speak.

In fact, barely a croak came out of her now as she took a final step toward him before she could turn left and escape into the tavern.

He had no right to treat her as if she was his. As if with one look, one caress, one whisper she'd fall into his arms.

What kind of woman did he think she was?

For heaven's sake, he didn't even know her true name.

She stepped out, about to veer left, but his stare, the way his mouth parted and his lower lip tugged with resistance, the way his nostrils flared slightly, as if he had something to say but was restraining himself, made her body disobey and come to a complete halt three feet in front of him.

"I was married once," he murmured. "A long time ago. It was painful to see her pass away."

The force of his words dropped like an anvil to her chest. Lord, he was married before? And she'd died?

She'd never heard any of his staff or friends even whisper the topic.

How old had he been?

Why did it happen?

What had his wife been like, and his marriage?

Her curiosity must have shown on her face, for his gaze flickered over her expression.

"I made a lot of mistakes with Elizabeth. I fear I'm making the same mistakes with you."

A lump ached in her throat. It grew bigger and bigger till she had to swallow past it to breathe.

His eyes reflected the pain he'd been through, whatever that had been, and however long it had lasted.

The tension between them stretched and stretched while neither spoke. Her chest heaved with the weight of his disclosure and the weight of her own emotions tripping like a tide through her.

And then the tinsmith, high atop a mare, came suddenly riding out from behind the stables, followed by another man in a brown hat she'd never seen before.

Caught off guard, she spun toward them, her long skirts shifting about her legs.

The tinsmith pulled back on his reins and addressed Harrison. "We thought we'd go check the docks. Maybe ride down the coast a ways."

To find the criminals?

"Take care of yourselves," Harrison told them. "That's the first thing that comes to mind, and last." He pointed toward east. "Billy and Michael headed toward the mountains, but if they don't pick up on any tracks, they're going to swing back toward Skagway."

"Shouldn't be too hard to track 'em," yelled the other fellow. "We figure they went down the coast by ship. Sailing out of here would be a lot quicker than hauling those animals on the trails."

Harrison's dark head tilted in contemplation of the man's words. "You never know. Seems to me they had everything planned carefully."

She knew why Harrison wasn't going after the men himself. There were no lawmen in town, and Harrison seemed to have a natural way of commanding authority. Two years on the run himself had made him an excellent marksman, as he'd demonstrated when showing her how to use the derringer under the bar.

At this point, the only things stolen were animals. The town itself was filled with people. People who needed protection and a sense of security. She understood his deep commitment to protect the folks in the tavern, and the people in town who might be comforted simply by his presence.

Maybe, she thought, he was even thinking of her protection.

Harrison gave them a salute and the men rode off. The clomp of hooves echoed through her rib cage, against the rapid beating of her heart.

When the men disappeared behind a cluster of trees, her lashes flew back to Harrison. "You think they'll find them?"

He turned his pensive face back to her, his dark cheeks smooth from a razor he'd put to them hours earlier. "Absolutely."

The conviction in his voice was soothing. Yet her heart came back to the topic of his late wife and the grief that he was struggling hard to hide.

Willa eyes stung with emotion. "Elizabeth must've been really something."

He nodded softly. His next words were barely audible, for he dropped the timbre of his voice. "Like you."

Willa's chest tightened as if a boa constrictor had wrapped itself around her and was squeezing hard.

"How did she pass away?"

"Trampled by horses."

Willa shuddered with the thought. "Were you with her?"

"No. But I should've been."

For a second, Willa clamped her eyes and turned her face to the ground.

"Twenty-one when I married. Foolish and stupid and thought love could save the world."

It can, she thought. Can't it?

When she looked back up again, his face was strained, his mouth quivering. He gulped and motioned with his hand to the stables, as if asking would she care for a walk to a more private place?

She didn't feel like parting company. She felt there was more to say between them. If only to tell him that this morning was a mistake and that she should have told him to leave immediately when he'd entered the spring room and caught her wearing next to nothing.

She turned and walked alongside him toward the outbuildings.

"I'm sorry about the door latch on the spring

room," he said quietly. "It's always been a loose lock. I thought the knob was stuck when I turned it and guess I pushed too hard."

She fumbled for a moment. "It slid right out of its socket."

He paused. "I'll get it fixed."

"You have more important things on your mind right now."

They reached the stable doors and she stepped through first. He followed, turning his broad shoulders past the narrow opening.

There was no one inside. Only the sweet smell of hay and the rustling of rabbits in the far corner.

Such serenity since the chaos hours earlier, when Chuck had been shot.

She leaned against the stall boards and watched a black rabbit munching on a fistful of fresh leaves. His mate, one with white-and-black spots with droopy ears, chewed on a carrot in the corner.

She sensed that Harrison didn't wish to speak. Maybe more words weren't coming easily to him. Maybe he'd open up and tell her the story of his wife when he was ready, she thought.

"I just came from Dr. Leighton's," she told him.

"How's Chuck?"

"Sleeping deeply. The doc says it's from the medicine. Said that Chuck might be out for days. The first few are always the worst, he said, till the body adjusts to the pain and the blood loss."

"I feel awful about what happened."

"It wasn't your fault. You were sleeping like the rest of us."

"Hmm," he mumbled, but she knew she wasn't convincing him.

He removed his Stetson and planted it on the stall boards. She pivoted her shoulder toward him and the hem of her skirts brushed his pant leg.

She felt the firm grip of his hand on her wrist. "Willa."

Her insides rumbled in warning, her dry lips stuck together.

He pulled her tighter toward him. Her boots shuffled on the straw.

"Willa," he said again, softly exploring the expression on her face.

When he drew her closer, she fell against his rock-solid chest. There was a look of something rough in his eyes. Something primal. Urgent.

He dropped her hand. It fell to her side. She was breathing heavy on his collar, his face and body arching toward her as if he wanted nothing more than to snatch every inch of clothing off her body.

With a heated groan, he pulled her into his arms and kissed her.

It was a deep, throbbing kiss that may have started on her lips, but the sensations rocked all of her senses.

She breathed in the scent of his skin. Heard the

crunching of straw beneath their feet. Tasted the essence of Harrison, became aware of the pressing of their bodies from rib to thigh and felt the overpowering desire to be with this man.

She kissed him back with the same urgency, loved the way their lips melded and the way he explored her with his mouth.

His head dropped and he kissed her throat, sending ripples through her. Without so much as touching her breasts, there seemed to be an invisible tie between every spot he kissed on her throat to the very tips of her nipples. Tugging, pulling, making her want more.

She didn't fear him.

This was a good man.

This was a man who cared about people. Who'd lost his first love and was perhaps aching for another. They were the same, then, weren't they? Two lonely souls yearning to be together, at this moment, in this place.

Harrison savored the feel of her throat, her earlobe, the sweet taste of her skin and the way her blond hair draped across her shoulders.

He was overwhelmed with the emotions that surged through him, the desire to fulfill her, the need to please Willa, the urgency to protect her and keep her safe from harm. He wanted to keep her here forever, just the two of them together and to hell with the rest of the world.

He wanted to please her, to show her there shouldn't be any fear between a man and woman when they were alone together. He wanted to ease her mind and her heart from whatever terror she'd experienced in Skagway.

Determined to go slowly, he slid his hands around her waist, up the back of her spine, felt the tightness of her rib cage beneath the fabric of her bodice. When he glanced down her neckline, he pleasured in the view of her bosom.

The swell of her golden breasts, half-revealed, firm and entrancing, were waiting to be touched.

She was a woman waiting to be touched. By him.

And there was the fine gold necklace twinkling up at him, teasing him with its secret resting spot between her breasts.

He moved his fingers across her throat, grazing her warm flesh as he picked up the chain to have a look at the hidden jewelry.

It was a medallion, still warm from her skin.

"A St. Christopher's medal," he said with appreciation. "The patron saint of travelers."

"Yes."

He lowered his face to her neckline, kissed along her flesh, loving the sounds of her moans and the sweet tug when she embedded her fingers in his hair.

She cupped her shoulders toward him, giving herself willingly with such allure it made his heart pound.

He tugged at the front button of her bodice.

Her eyes flashed up into his and for a moment, he thought she would object.

She hesitated for a moment, but didn't withdraw from his touch. Hallelujah.

With the eagerness of an adolescent on his first time, he undid another button and another and another. Her corset revealed itself, a pretty lavender color that flashed against her creamy skin and golden hair.

"You're stunning."

He watched her ribs move up and down with her rapid breathing, enraptured by the beautiful symmetry of her breasts, moving slightly and making his body respond with all the lust of a red-blooded male.

His erection grew harder. The heat of his blood pounded through every muscle. The hairs on his neck seemed to come alive, bristling to attention, and even the breath in his lungs seemed thicker and more arduous to push in and out.

Where would this end?

Did it have to?

"Willa."

"Mmm."

"Come with me."

"Where?" She looked up into his face, her features gentle and relaxed.

"Do you trust me?"

"Yes. But I can't…at least I don't think I can…do what you obviously want to." Her soft voice lowered to a hush. "It would be my first time."

Just as he'd suspected. A virgin. But one he wouldn't push. A sense of guilt overtook him, quickly washed away by the look of happiness in her eyes, in the tender way she reached up and touched his jaw, as though giving her consent to his advances. To a point.

He took her hand and led her down the center aisle. "Come with me."

With her dress unbuttoned and her breasts partially revealed, she followed him with all the admiration and respect in her expression that he could've hoped for, that day when she'd walked into his bar holding the sign for Bartender Wanted and in such dire straits that she could trust no one.

Now, he felt the weight of her trust as he led her into the private alcove of his office.

When they entered, Harrison turned the lock in the key and spun around to Willa.

She was breathless, corset exposed, her medallion glistening, and standing in front of his scratched pine desk with such grace that he could barely resist her.

Morning sunlight filtered in through the narrow ribbons of glass at the top of the rafters. A wall-size bookshelf behind her contained a few maps of Alaska, a veterinarian's manual and a registry for the comings and goings of the livestock he took in.

The interior walls were open at the very top, twelve feet above them. It allowed them to hear footsteps if someone was approaching through the stables, or the murmur of horses and cattle if there were any inside.

But there weren't.

There was just Harrison and Willa.

Anticipation was trapped in her eyes.

"I won't hurt you," he promised.

"I believe that now."

"I want you to know that I find you—" he stepped closer, taking her into his arms and pressing her against the desk "—irresistible."

He kissed her cheek, followed her jawline to her temple, to her ear, to the back of her neck.

His hands roved her body. When he slid open the button at her waistline, he was pleasantly surprised to find the bodice and skirt were connected in a dress, and that it parted easily around her hips.

Gasping at his touch, she reached up and trailed her hands across his shoulders, knotting her warm fingers at the back of his neck, making the ribbon of muscles on his stomach contract wildly. His body tensed and swelled with all the restraint of a powerless man.

All of his thoughts were centered on Willa and what she might want out of this situation. How she might like to be held and kissed and soothed. There was more than one way to give her pleasure, and he dearly ached to show her.

Chapter Eleven

Harrison waited for a few seconds in the privacy of his office, wondering if Willa would tell him to stop his advances. But she looked at him with clear eyes and a soft smile.

"Maybe this isn't what you want." A dash of guilt rushed through him again, quickly dispelled by her encouragement.

"We'll go slow, won't we?" she murmured, running her hands up his shirt, over the muscles of his chest. "You'll stop if I ask you."

"Hmm." He nodded gently in absolute agreement.

He tugged at the top lace of her corset. It parted and her breasts spilled out. Not enough to display her nipples, just enough to make his mouth water and his eyes fill with a bountiful feast.

He pulled another lace. It, too, parted and fell open. And this time, it exposed the left edge of pink areola. The one he'd been daydreaming about since this morning when he'd seen them wet.

He fingered the third tie of her corset, but it was snug and required a harder tug. He gave it a pull and was well rewarded when both breasts spilled out, their soft virginal nipples grazing the fragrant air. So lush, large and wondrous.

He scooped one in his palm, marveling at the weight and the curve of her flesh.

Willa gazed at him with such tenderness, his immediate reaction was to bend down and kiss her breast. And then the other. Supple and warm.

She boldly reached for his shirt and unbuttoned it, starting from the bottom. When she got to the final one at the top, she parted the fabric and slid her hands inside.

Oh, the pleasure of her touch.

In a bold move of his own, he swiped everything off his desk—the ledger, the leather desk pad, the box of lead pencils. He slid his arms behind her back and under her seat, picked her up, smiling at her small yelp, and laid her upon the pine. Her dress parted. His pulse leaped.

He undid her corset completely, and pulled down her pantaloons over her slender thighs and off her wiggling toes.

He could gaze at her naked body forever. Starting with the rapt face that held so many feelings he couldn't read them all. He did see wonder there, too, and sexuality as smoldering as his own, and curiosity and sheer splendor in the wonder of being together.

His focus trailed down the dips of her throat, the soft beating pulse, the breasts shaped like the beautiful clay form of some Greek goddess, down the undulating ribs, her belly button and the light curls at her thighs.

Not wanting to scare her, but knowing he could not resist her—resist this—he stepped between her legs, slid his hands one along each soft thigh, parted her legs and dipped his head to kiss her stomach.

She pulled back, probably unsure what he was doing and what he wanted.

He kissed her knee. "I'll stop if you say. I only want to make you feel good."

Her forehead was furrowed with concern. An expression of mixed emotions raced across her face, but at his gentle words, she smiled shyly, looked to the ceiling, arched her eyebrows as if privately shocked at what they were doing, while at the same time fighting laughter, indicating she was also incredibly pleased.

He laughed softly, enjoying the fact that he was her first, that he would show her how caring he could be.

She relaxed her legs, her thighs slackening beneath his palms.

The scent of soap from this morning was still on her skin.

He kissed and licked and flicked his tongue along the crevice of her hip and thigh, smiling when she moaned and moved her knee slightly, as if sending a silent invitation that this was all right with her, that she understood what he wanted and that she wanted it, too.

He kneeled beneath her, his knees finding a patch of straw on the stone floor, his lips finding her sweetness.

He parted her tenderly with his fingertips, then flicked his tongue over the moistness. He heard her audible gasp. A feeling of contentment surged through him at the sound of Willa. He lingered on one side of her, then the other, then found the button on the top and explored it gently.

She wiggled beneath his grasp, moving in rhythm to his tongue. He loved the taste. He loved the sensation of being with her. When he sensed that she was near the brink, he slipped his tongue inside. She rode his mouth to orgasm, moving her hips up and down, allowing him the sweet torture of anticipation for himself, forcing him to ride out his own primitive urges while he satisfied hers.

Oh, the glory. She arched upward, then down, then froze, then rode him again. Everlasting pleasure.

When her waves subsided, he kissed his way up her belly.

She laughed softly.

It was the most delicious sound.

He kissed his way up her breast, then the other, then her throat and landed at her lips.

She kissed like a goddess. His erection strained against the fabric of his jeans. When she reached down timidly toward his leg, he moved away slightly.

"This moment is for you."

"But I thought I could just touch you. I thought you expected—"

"No expectations." He watched the glimmer of daylight shine through the planks of the wall, beautiful shadows of light and shade glimmering over her breasts, and one golden ray catching the soft curve of her upper lip. "Believe me, it was already incredible for me, without you doing any more. Watching you. Holding you. Knowing that you liked this. You did like it, didn't you, darlin'?"

Willa's heart was still pounding from the glorious burst of intimacy she'd just shared with Harrison. He was kneeling beside her head as she lay on his desk. His dark hair was mussed up by what her fingers had done while he was making love to her—for what else was it but that?

"It was amazing, Harrison. I didn't know you could get that much feeling out of me."

He brushed the side of her cheek. "Well worth it, then, for me, too."

Their time together had been more tender and more raw than she'd ever expected. He'd been so careful to ensure her pleasure before his.

She wanted him to continue, wanted to feel Harrison making love to her in the full sense of the word. But she could see by the look of determination in his eyes that it wouldn't happen today. Even so, this moment with him had been like a seismic shift in her life. It went contrary to everything she'd feared might happen the first time she was with a man. There was nothing to fear from Harrison.

A bead of perspiration appeared on his brow and soaked the side of his temples.

He stood up and began to dress.

She marveled at the splendor of his body. His un-buttoned shirt parted open, and she caught a glimpse of the scars she'd seen this morning in the spring room.

What battles had he fought, this gentle man? She'd have to ask him. For now, she focused on the yards of golden muscles, the slight matting of hair, the slick abdomen and the triangular shape of hair that went lower and lower.

She sat up on the desk, pulled him toward her and ran her hands up the smooth sides of his ribs.

He parted slightly from her, lowered his head and kissed the tip of her breast, making her stomach do another drastic somersault.

"Willa," he whispered simply. Her name, uttered

from his lips, never felt more true and honest than in the privacy of this moment.

She was Willa. Would always be Willa to him.

Harrison wasn't a big talker, she noticed. He was a man of action more than words, and she admired him for that. He took a step back to give her space to dress. She clasped the ends of her corset together in order to do up the front laces.

He asked with a gentle grin, "May I do it?"

Flushed with the excitement of what they'd done together, the surprising amount of sentiment they'd expressed, she nodded and removed her fingers from her corset.

Her breasts were still exposed. Standing between her legs, he smiled at the sight. He kissed each breast as he covered them with her lavender corset and tied the laces. He certainly did like to kiss her there.

It was such an intimate gesture to have him dressing her, head bowed, fully concentrating.

He grazed her skin as he reached for her St. Christopher medal and held it between his tanned fingers. "Did someone give you this?"

"It was the only thing passed down from my mother."

"She's protecting you on your journey in Alaska." He nestled the medallion snugly between her breasts and reached for the first button of her bodice.

"How long were you married?"

"Two years."

Willa sighed. So young to be gone. Elizabeth had been robbed of life before she'd barely gotten started.

"She must be happy, wherever she is, that she got to spend at least two years with you."

His mouth tugged at one corner, which made her feel silly that she'd said it. It was simplistic. Something a child might say. How could she comfort him? What could she possibly say to alleviate the pain?

"What did you mean earlier, when you said you might be making the same mistakes with me?"

His lips moved tighter, but he kept his head bowed as he finished the buttons on her skirts. "I fear for your life."

"You're scared? For me?"

Finishing with her clothes, he took a step back. "From the day you walked in and told me someone was after you."

"But he's not after me. Not anymore. You don't have to worry."

"When you go out for a ride, I worry that you'll fall. When it's raining and you go for a walk on the boardwalk, I fear you'll slip. When you serve a man at the bar and he so much as looks at you in a menacing—"

She reared back in absolute surprise and he stopped himself from finishing.

"Never mind. My…thoughts aren't important."

But they were important. She didn't think he paid

much attention to what she was doing. Let alone that he was watching out for her.

As he buttoned his own shirt, she placed a hand on his to stop him. She trailed the swollen red patches of scarred tissue on his ribs.

"What happened?"

"I stepped into an oncoming knife."

"From who?"

"Someone who was trying to intimidate a woman."

"Did they succeed?"

"No. My brother and I caught the whole gang."

"Do you always come to the aid of damsels in distress?"

"Only the special ones." His lips tugged with warm amusement. "How do you feel?"

"After you attacked me?" she teased.

"Yeah." He grinned.

"Mighty good."

"Me, too." He kissed her on the cheek, then the lips. It was a soft kiss, one that revealed the pleasure he'd gotten from their time together. But it brought out the nervousness she was trying to subdue tingling under her skin.

She was playing with danger, being intimate with the boss. With a man who made no promises. Is that the type of woman she wanted to be? She touched her golden necklace and thought of her mother. Is that the type of woman her mother would want her to be?

Willa reached up and tucked the straggling hair behind his ear. She was content to be with him. In fact, blissfully so. Miles from home, she was a woman free to do as she pleased.

Willa wasn't alone with Harrison again for days. At least, not for any length of time that they could discuss anything personal. However, as she worked the lunch hour, then took a couple of hours off for a stroll down the boardwalk, then back again to evening duties, she was well aware there was a difference between them.

Harrison's expression was gentler, and at times mischievous, as he passed her drinks across the bar, or teased her about mixing up a sandwich order, or remarked on what a lovely blouse she was wearing.

She blushed each time. Did anyone else notice how flustered she got around him? Did anyone else sense the innuendos in his tone, or God forbid, had anyone seen or heard anything about their time together in the stables?

Apparently not.

She was trying to make sense of it, her newfound freedom with her body, the undeniably crazy lust she felt toward him, the shyness still at what they'd done together and her curiosity about the act itself.

Still, it didn't help to dwell on the subject, for she had work to accomplish. Not being alone with him was partly on purpose, on her end, anyway, because she hadn't yet decided where she fit into Harrison's life. Where she wished to fit. Or how much of herself she wanted to expose. The conversations, the private smiles, the charming way he had of listening to her opinion on things, were comforting enough, for the moment. She felt as though she was getting to know him on a subtle new level. And she liked what she saw.

Three nights after their interlude, well past eleven o'clock and working behind the bar, Harrison smiled as he recalled his intimate time with Willa.

He poured a glass of ale from the keg, turned and delivered it to the banker at the counter.

"Much obliged," said the gent, tipping his bowler hat.

Harrison poured another one for a different customer, while eyeing Willa across the room as she delivered drinks to the crowd. Her dark blouse and skirt whirled as she turned and reached, accentuating her fine curves, and making his pulse quicken.

What was it that he wanted from their courtship?

More of the same? Perhaps going even further next time?

A tide of guilt crept up his neck and made him tug at his collar. He never would've treated Elizabeth this way. When he was young, he had insisted on marriage before the marriage bed.

Now that he was older and had experienced more

in life, was it fair to simply take from a woman that which he couldn't resist, without promising more of himself, without committing to anything deeper, or morally right?

Other women he'd been with in the past few years had never made him stop to think about it. Willa, however…Willa was different. Or should he say *he* was different when he was with her? There hadn't been that strike of loneliness the morning after.

Had it been a fluke?

Would he feel emptier if they spent another interlude together, and another and another? Perhaps she would wear out on him like the other passing women had.

Another pang of guilt for even thinking about Willa like this made his jaw tighten.

Their morning together had been a far cry from his usual. Not only in terms of spending time with her, kissing her entire body like he had, but also on the other side of the spectrum, the sadness he'd felt at Chuck's injury and the continual outrage at the livestock theft.

Some blasted criminal had masterminded the operation. Had to have. Otherwise why pick Harrison's stables? Common thieves would pillage a weary traveler on the road. Not a well-guarded stable in a community surrounded by able-bodied men.

Someone had definitely scouted his business and had made their move.

Harrison hadn't heard any news yet from Billy. The tinsmith, unfortunately, had returned the same night he'd left, saying they'd uncovered nothing, and that he didn't have more time to follow the trail due to having to get back to his work and his shop.

No one else had sighted any suspects in the district, either, nor had there been any more thefts.

Harrison would bide his time and wait for the information to come in. Sooner or later, some decent man somewhere would report the stench of a criminal in hiding.

Two working men walked into the bar, but Harrison didn't pay them much attention. Willa came up beside him, businesslike and proper, not even daring to look at him behind the bar.

He got a kick out of that. All evening, she was trying to ignore him so that perhaps that sweet blush of hers wouldn't give her away to the patrons.

Harrison had been trying to avoid her these past three days, too, saying not much more than "good morning" and "fine day" when others were watching them. Both he and Willa had been so busy attending to their duties to Chuck, unloading tavern supplies and calming the guests, that Harrison had felt that she needed time in the evenings to do her work.

However, maybe both had stepped away from each other because both were doubting what to do next. What was to follow that unbelievably passionate morning?

Harrison watched as Willa walked to the back of the tavern and served her ale. Her skirts flounced around her ankles, her brown blouse with its lacy ruffle danced across her breasts.

Cheerfully, she turned around with a tray full of mugs, looked at the burly man seated against the back wall, dropped her tray to the floor and screamed.

Glass crashed, heads whipped around, Harrison jumped with alarm and Willa backed away from the grinning man in a tight leather vest and white shirt that barely covered his large gut.

Who the hell was he?

The entire room waited in silence.

Blood drained pale from her face as she gritted her teeth. "Keenan Crawford. You black-toothed pig."

Chapter Twelve

Willa stared at the thick lips, the square forehead and the smug smile on the brute's face. Crawford *was* a pig. Even the way he sneered at her made her body shake and her bones chill.

He was seated next to his right-hand man, Owen Price, leaner and five years younger than forty-year-old Crawford. Willa had often bumped into Price at the butcher shop, but the man never spoke to her directly, always lurked in the background.

Dressed in an ill-fitting shirt and wool trousers, the butcher rolled up his sleeves as though he was about to hammer some meat. "Evenin', Mary. Or should I say Willa?"

Her face caught fire. Wisps of hair clung with sticky moisture to her neck.

His calm composure was terrifying. With a bulbous nose and thick neck jutting out of a too-tight collar, he winked at her.

She felt sick.

At some point around her, the voices of the crowd had stopped. Silence permeated the heavy air. Everyone ceased what they were doing and heads turned in her direction.

The two barmaids were picking up the scattered glass behind Willa, God bless them, but Willa couldn't move for the fear that rooted her to the floorboards.

The man had found her and she trembled for what that might mean. The brutality of the way he'd treated her the last time she'd seen him brought a wave of nausea to her throat. He'd tried to rape her, this pig, and yet he sat here expecting to be served and pretending he was welcome.

She shuddered with indignation and anger, then wondered what she had to fear.

How could he snatch her from here? There were witnesses and he wouldn't dare come near her. But he likely did know where she lived, upstairs in the tavern, and he could come back again and again to torment her.

"How did you find me?"

"The ocean has eyes."

"This man tried to kill me," she said softly to the listening crowd, to the familiar faces she'd come to know and trust in the weeks she'd been here.

Gasps went out.

Two miners to her right rose to their feet. "Leave her alone, mister."

"Does it look like I want to kill her?" said the butcher. He turned back to Willa. "You've mistaken me for someone else. I've only come to say hello."

Firm footsteps brushed the floor behind her, then Harrison stood towering beside her, closer to Crawford than she was. Harrison had taken to wearing his guns ever since Chuck's shooting, and she was grateful for it.

"Now that you've said hello," Harrison said to Crawford. "I'd appreciate it if you'd say goodbye."

The crowd snickered.

Crawford's nose turned red. His mouth clenched into an ugly tight circle. "Ah, the boss man."

Harrison shoulders stiffened. "Get up real slow, then get out real quick."

"You tell 'em, Harrison." An old man in the far corner who'd been drinking for the past hour let out a hoot of laughter.

Price rearranged his shoulders in the chair beside his boss, stretching out his legs, exposing his holstered guns and flexing his right hand over one of his six-shooters, letting everyone know he was armed and ready.

The butcher's nostrils flared. His damp eyes narrowed at Harrison. "I paid for a drink I didn't finish yet."

Willa looked to Crawford's mug of ale, three-quarters full. Sarah must've served him.

"I'll put the money toward the spilled drinks you caused." Harrison motioned to the wet floor. His hands didn't move toward the holstered guns at his sides, but Willa watched Crawford's eyes drop to Harrison's weapons.

Price stood up and snarled through crooked lips, protecting his boss. "You don't know who you're dealing with. A prominent citizen from Skagway. One of the most successful businessmen in town."

Harrison scowled. "Doesn't sound that successful to me. Holding a gun to a woman's head seems kind of desperate."

The crowd went quiet again, likely wondering what Harrison meant.

In that instant, Willa could see it in the mossy black eyes that Crawford *knew* she'd told Harrison the story of the attempted forced marriage.

Maybe the butcher felt betrayed by her telling it, or maybe he was outraged that people in the bar were snickering at him, or maybe he was just vile, through and through, for he lunged forward off his chair, lickety-split, and swung at Harrison.

"Ugh," muttered Willa in surprise, whipped in the shoulder by flinging arms and legs.

She scooted out of the way and stepped back under the ring of lanterns on the ceiling.

Crawford's fist plowed into Harrison's gut.

Harrison toppled backward. They fell onto a table. Drinks crashed. Women screamed. Men hollered.

Price went to leap onto Harrison as well, but Shamus came up out of nowhere and cocked his gun to Price's temple.

"Easy, mister."

Price's eyes rolled to the side of his head, where the barrel was pointing, and he slowly lifted his arms into the air.

The crowd reared back and watched the fight.

"Get him, Harrison!"

"Pound him in the ribs!"

"Stop!" Willa shouted in between the brutality, rubbing her sore shoulder. "Stop it, both of you!"

The men continued wrestling and punching. "Crawford, get out!" she screamed.

Harrison, who'd been knocked to the table, lifted his boot and kicked Crawford, who was making another run at him, squarely in the chest. Crawford was thrown back into the crowd, the onlookers leaped away and Crawford came back swinging harder than ever.

Harrison ducked a punch, then gave one of his own. Willa heard the crunch of knuckles on jawbone.

Both men reeled from the impact.

Crawford's eyes throbbed with the intent of murder, she could see it as plain as day, but Harrison kept coming. Crawford lunged, got his hands around Harrison's throat and, to her horror, Harrison's face turned red. She leaped forward to kick the animal, but Harrison kneed Crawford's gut. Crawford let go and doubled over for a second, long enough for Harrison to pound his shoulders.

The butcher fell to his knees, dazed, bloodied, panting for air.

Harrison wiped the blood off his lip with the back of his shirtsleeve. He stepped back, alongside Willa, to watch his assailant teeter from side to side. As though he were a great tree and someone would soon shout *timber.*

"Had enough, mister?" Shamus hollered. "Or do you get the message?"

Spit and blood drizzled from the butcher's mouth. His heavy breathing continued. Then, with a look so vicious and bloodthirsty at Harrison that it made Willa's heart turn upside down, the giant man held the back of an empty chair and struggled to his feet.

"By whatever way you got here," Harrison growled, "get out."

Crawford bit down on the fury threatening to engulf him as he stumbled to his feet to get a good long look at the man he would surely kill, one day soon.

Harrison Rowlan.

Tavern owner and nothing more than a lowly beetle in the scheme of things. He was the type of man who sounded good in front of his friends—

when he knew he had help to back him up—but as soon as Crawford got Rowlan alone, he'd whimper like all the others had.

Don't hurt me, sir.

I'll do anything you say, sir.

Crawford looked to the woman. Her trembling made it all worthwhile. To feel her cower was to feel her succumb to him in bed. Women. All whimpering nothings till he laid his hands on them.

He spit out a mouthful of blood on the floor, looked to Price, who still had a gun trained on him by the one they called the bouncer, and stalked through the open door.

Cool air hit him in the face. A night breeze from the ocean slapped his skin, dried his sweat and made him hunger for just one minute alone with Rowlan to dunk the son of a bitch's head under the weight of that ocean water and watch him squirm for oxygen, then grow limp with death.

"Sorry, boss." Price rushed to keep up to Crawford's long stabilizing stride. "Wasn't anything I could do to help back there. But I'm not leaving this town till he gets what's comin'."

"That's for damn sure."

They made their way through the dark sleeping streets, toward the horses they'd hitched by the water several hours earlier.

No one even suspected that he, Crawford, master of this damn place they called Alaska, had already sold the donkey, horse and two dairy cows to some lame farmer south of Skagway. Ten times the price of any beast back home.

Rowlan.

Crawford cursed the name. Now he knew why Mary Somerset had settled here. It was her goddamn boss who'd set his sights on *her.* Crawford could tell the man had feelings for her in one second flat by the looks that passed between them.

Boss, indeed.

If the son of a bitch wasn't sleeping with her already, he wanted to.

Well, he couldn't have her.

She was Crawford's bride.

Not only because she was a looker, and at how good she'd felt pressed between Crawford's legs, but also because she'd been exposed to a private conversation between him and his men.

She didn't seem to realize it, but she'd overheard clues of who he was and just how far his masterminding went in the district. If he married her, he could control her. If he didn't make her his wife, he'd have no choice but to deal with her in another way.

"You all right?" Harrison cupped his arm around Willa's waist and, with a nod to Shamus, headed for the kitchen to the back gardens. He ignored the surprised looks on some of his customers' faces at how familiar he was being with Willa.

Willa nodded. She rubbed her sore right shoulder and his concerns multiplied.

"You sure?"

"I got bumped, but I'll be fine."

His knuckles ached from the fistfight, but he ignored the minor irritation. They stepped past the two cooks who were standing and staring at them in the hallway.

"Are you okay, honey?" asked Natalie.

Willa nodded.

Harrison watched her inhale. When some of the color came back to her face, the tension within him subsided.

They stepped past the counters in the kitchen. Both fireplaces were lit and crackling. George and Natalie entered behind them and took their places behind the stoves and boiling pots of potatoes.

"He found me," Willa whispered.

"Doesn't matter," Harrison reassured her. "You're safe here. Almost everyone in town got a good look at him and know he's dangerous. We stick together in Eagle's Cliff and look after our own. You're one of us."

She gave him a shaky smile.

"I signaled Shamus to follow Crawford and see where he goes. Shamus took another man with him."

"Thank you."

Harrison tried to soothe her fears. "He can't get to you. My room's just down the hall from yours. I'd like you to take the derringer from the bar and keep it at your bedside. I'll get another one for the tavern."

She nodded, unhooking herself from his fingers as they reached the back door. "That would make me feel better."

They stepped out into the night air. He gulped nice and slow, ran his hand down her back and let his fingers sink to her waist.

She stepped onto the grass path and wove her way beneath the trees. Moonlight skimmed the roof of the stables and lit the top of her golden hair.

A frown furrowed her brow. "Sorry to get you involved with this."

"You didn't cause that man to be violent. He did that all on his own."

"He called me Mary."

"Mary." Harrison rolled it over on his lips. "Mary." He smiled wistfully at the pretty name, yet the disclosure of her true name made him feel distanced from her, at how little he knew about her true identity.

"Mary Willa Somerset," she admitted.

Harrison splayed his palm over his chest. "It's got a nice ring to it."

"My uncle used to call me Willa when I was a child, and I liked it. It means fierce defender."

"You are fierce."

He was glad to see her unexpected smile.

"Where'd the Banks come from?"

"A play name. A friend and I used to pretend we were lady pirates on the high seas."

A cool breeze kicked up and ruffled through his hair. "I wouldn't mind being taken by a lady pirate."

Her warm brown eyes glimmered in the moonlight. "I'd hold you hostage and never let you go."

"That sounds interesting."

"Thank you for what you did back there," she whispered, stepping up on tiptoe to embrace him.

She gave him a kiss. It was sweet and gentle and arousing.

But they were in a public place. Folks were likely peeking out windows to watch them. He pulled away, more for her reputation than his own.

She blinked up at him and he could see she was trying to read his motivations.

"There might be folks watching."

"Ah," she said, nodding toward the tavern, but he wondered, by her ruffled expression, if she felt there was another reason.

She grew shaky again, her lips downturned as she stared off into the distant mountains, deep in thought and looking past him almost as if he weren't here.

"Willa?" He touched her shoulder. "What exactly did Crawford do to you?"

Her head jerked back toward him. "He tried to force me to…to marry him."

But there was something more, something frightening she wasn't telling him.

"And?" he coaxed. "I'd like to hear what else is bothering you. You don't have to face this alone. You can tell me."

She crossed her arms and hugged them against her chest. With a hesitant shift of her shoulders, she spoke softly into the wind. "He tried to rape me."

Harrison slumped backward as if someone had punched him in the gut. His blood pounded at Crawford's audacity to take a seat at Harrison's tavern and taunt Willa the way he had, and now this.

Harrison was afraid something like this may have happened to her, but not surprised after he'd met the butcher face-to-face and had seen the kind of a person the man was.

Harrison bridged the distance to Willa, sliding his arm around her shoulders and pressing her against his chest. "I'm sorry you had to go through that. I asked you the day we met if he hurt you, but maybe you couldn't tell me then. Did he?"

He waited in heated silence, livid with the man who'd take advantage of a young woman.

"No," she said into his shirt. "He never got that far."

"He never will."

Willa turned her face upward. The moon skimmed her eyelashes and tinged the outline of her pretty lips.

"You have so many problems to worry about, Harrison." She looked to the stables. "It appears that Chuck is on the mend, but there's no word on your stolen livestock. Where do you suppose the law is? And your brother? You sent for them three days ago."

"I was wondering the same thing."

They embraced for a few moments longer till he turned and urged her back inside. He convinced her to call it a night since it was past midnight already. He located the derringer behind the bar, took it up to her room and ensured she was well secured before he left her side.

He finished the rest of his duties, quietly fuming at the butcher who dared show his face tonight.

Harrison had his hands full. On one side, he was looking for the horse thieves and discouraging folks from boarding their animals in his stables till he could provide proper security again. He pointed them instead to the livery stables the blacksmith ran, but Harrison couldn't keep that up forever since he was losing income.

On the other side, there was the dangerous situation with Willa.

Harrison paced the floor of his tavern long after everyone cleared out and he locked the doors. He was waiting for an answer from Shamus and wondering which way to turn, since he was shorthanded with Billy out of town and Chuck out of commission. Harrison was short not only by two hardworking stable hands, but unbeknownst to most folks in town when he'd hired the well-trained young men, he was also short by two hired gunmen. He waited and waited for word, but the wind howled outside, and as the fireplace along the back wall ebbed, the room got colder.

There was no way on earth Harrison could go to bed and fall asleep till he heard where the butcher was spending *his* night.

Chapter Thirteen

It was two-thirty in the morning when a rider pounded on the tavern door. Harrison, unable to sleep or rest, bounded from behind the bar, where he was restocking fresh kegs of ale, to let him in. Ceiling lanterns shone down on the polished bar top, gleaming from a fresh oiling Harrison had given it an hour earlier.

"Are you Harrison Rowlan?" The man wore guns. Roughly thirty, he tilted the brim of his Stetson. The wind blew at his hair. A scruff of dark shadows lined his jaw.

"Yes."

"I'm Justin Baker. I work on the Stafford ranch." The man extended his hand and they shook.

"Your man Shamus sent me with a message. Said to tell you Crawford and his man are headed back to Skagway."

"By horse?"

"They boarded their horses on ship and sailed south."

"Where's Shamus?"

"He stayed behind to get more information from the dockyards. Everything's quiet, though. Most men are sleeping. I imagine he'll be along shortly."

"Thanks for the message. Care to come in to rest, or have something to eat?"

"I've got a bunk at the Stafford ranch. Today was my day off but I've gotta work tomorrow. Thanks all the same."

"Whenever you have a chance to swing by, meal and drinks are on me."

They shook again and the man left.

Harrison went back to the bar, taking comfort in the new six-shooter he'd put on the shelf beside the cash drawer.

Thirty minutes later, Shamus appeared. Alone. He'd sent the other man who rode with him home to bed.

"Didn't get any more information," said Shamus, his eyes rimmed with a need for sleep. "But the two fishermen I did speak to say the sailing ship they left on was definitely headed to Skagway. They know the captain."

The coastline trail to Skagway that the horses would have to take was rocky and narrow, full of crags and possible missteps. That's why most travel between the two harbors happened by ship.

"That's good news," said Harrison, although his

stomach remained unsettled. If Crawford had come once to make trouble for Willa, he could come again.

Shamus left. Harrison locked the doors. He snuffed out the lanterns, went up to bed, kept his room door slightly ajar and slept in his clothes.

Word from Quinn finally came in at seven the next morning, before Willa was finished with her breakfast. Harrison had already explained to her the information he had about Crawford leaving by ship. She was relieved but still wary.

George and Natalie were busy baking in the background.

Harrison took the note from the messenger, a young boy from the docks who'd come to the kitchen door to deliver it, and read it alone in the bar.

Harrison, I'm sorry I can't be there. I'm held up by a court case. Can't leave for a couple of days yet. I gave your information to Deputy Marshal Langford, but he's held up on the same case. He put his deputies onto your livestock theft, but even that has to be added to the others waiting in line. Will notify you of any news, otherwise see you in three to four days. Hang tight.
Quinn.

Hell. There were so many horse and cattle thefts, Harrison had to wait in a lineup for the law to even get to his.

Jackson Langford, the new deputy marshal of Skagway who'd only come into the position two months ago, was a solid friend of both his and Quinn's. The three of them had worked together for the past two years to get *all* of their faces off the Wanted posters. Jackson had been targeted just like Harrison for speaking up against the crooked former deputy marshal. Two months ago when they'd finally apprehended the ruthless lawman who was behind the vigilante gangs, the murders and robberies, Jackson had replaced him as deputy marshal.

Too bad those hadn't been the only gangs centered in Skagway. Because the district had been virtually lawless for the past two years, the livestock crime rings were now thriving.

Harrison tucked the note into his pocket and tried to swallow his disappointment. He needed to think clearly to produce his own plan of action.

Was he supposed to sit here and wait while the thieves got farther and farther away?

What about Billy and Michael? They hadn't sent any word yet, which meant they had no news about spotting the criminals or the stolen animals.

He returned to the kitchen and sat beside Willa at the table. She bit into a slice of buttered rye bread. Her hair was wet from a bath she'd taken upon wakening. "What happened, Harrison? What did the note say?"

"My brother will be here in three to four days,

when his court case is over. And the deputy marshal's aware of my stolen property."

"Aware?" She frowned, a gentle pull of confusion furrowing her brow. "Is he on his way?"

"Seems like I'm not the only one with livestock troubles."

She set down the rye bread on her half-eaten plate of eggs and touched his arm. "That's not what you wanted to hear."

Her way of comforting sat easy on him.

"More coffee?" Natalie, in a bright blue apron, squeezed her round frame from behind a stack of pie plates. "Harrison?" She held the tin pot over the table.

"Sure."

She poured then looked awkwardly to Willa. "Mary? Or, um, Willa? Mary, I guess, it is. Sorry."

Willa's cheeks looked as though they'd struck a match. "Please, Willa is fine. Truly. My uncle used to call me Willa."

Natalie brightened, as if connecting with Willa again. "He called you Willa Banks?"

Willa, flustered, wove her fingers into the buttons of her blouse. "Mary Willa Somerset."

"Ah," said Natalie, her posture stiffening once more. She was polite, but definitely confused by the situation. Perhaps even hurt that Willa had given them a false name.

Harrison wasn't fully over the name change himself, but he'd understood it from the beginning. He'd told her outright the day they met that he suspected the name Willa Banks wasn't her true name. Perhaps that's why he wasn't taking things as personally as Natalie and George.

George was off in his corner, stirring pudding over the fire. He hadn't said a word to Willa this morning, not in Harrison's presence, anyway, simply stuck to his baking of scones and pies. He wasn't even humming, as he often did when he baked.

Harrison hoped Willa didn't notice George's retreat, but her eyes fluttered in the old cook's direction, and she stiffly took another sip of coffee.

Things didn't go much better that afternoon, when they opened for lunchtime. Only half the usual customers showed up. Oddly, they were all men. Not a single woman.

Harrison tried to keep focused on his work, tried to keep his spirits up for Willa's sake, but neither had much to do today. Customers were few and far between.

In the afternoon, he asked Shamus to cover for them, then suggested to Willa they go visit Chuck at the doctor's house.

She clapped her hands in delight. "I'd like to see him."

They were both pleasantly surprised to find the man sitting up in bed and eating soup.

"Feeling better?" Harrison removed his Stetson as Willa sat on the chair beside the bed.

Chuck's hair was messed up from spending so much time on his back, but his face had good color. "My head's still not clear, but the doc says it won't get better till I'm off the morphine."

They spent half an hour with him, till his eyes started to drift off, before returning back to the unusually quiet tavern.

"Something going on in town I don't know about?" Harrison asked the banker sitting at the bar, around five.

"No, sir. But I heard there was quite a commotion in here last night."

"Right," said Harrison, but he didn't indulge in further gossip.

The evening crowd wasn't much bigger. The following afternoon Harrison finally got wind of the reason why, after spending another day of slow traffic.

"My Bessie begged me not to come in here today," one of the regulars, a postal clerk, said as he took a stool at the bar and ordered a drink. "But I told her no woman's gonna stand in the way of me and my beer."

Mr. Beatty waltzed in next, the old guy with the big mouth who was now renting a room from someone else. "It's all over town. You've got some woman in here goes by some other name than what we know her by. Some crazed man is after her, and the ladies in town are stopping their men from patronizing your tavern."

Unfortunately, the loudmouth said it as Willa was stepping out of the kitchen with a tray of sandwiches.

She lowered her head, delivered the food, then poured drinks for the gents along the far wall, but Harrison knew she'd overheard.

At closing time, she whispered to Harrison, "I've turned into a liability for you."

"Don't be silly." He turned around and squeezed her hand behind the bar. A flare of need and desire shot through him. It'd been so long since he'd been able to touch her, it seemed.

"That's why we haven't had one female customer in here since the brawl."

"It'll change. They'll see that you're still the charming, honest person they know."

"*Honest?* That's not what they think. They think I've deceived them. And if I wasn't working for you, Crawford wouldn't have come and you wouldn't have fought."

"The news will die down and customers will come back."

"I'm putting you in danger with Crawford."

"What danger? He's gone."

Harrison wanted to reach out and embrace her. Wanted to stroke her shoulders and tell her that all would be fine as long as she was with him. But he didn't dare take a step toward her in front of these spectators, otherwise they'd have more ammunition against Willa. That she was involved with her boss as well as some lunatic butcher from Skagway. That maybe the two men were fighting over her and that's what all the fuss was about.

But seeing her in such distress, rubbing her temples and working hard to smile and make conversation with folks who secretly questioned who she was and what else she might be concealing, made Harrison speak the truth to her at closing time. She had the right to know what was on his mind, and to make her own decisions.

"One of my guests came in with a broodmare today."

She slapped empty mugs onto the bar as the last of the guests filtered out. "Yes, I heard. He's boarding her at the blacksmith's. Where you've been sending the animals of all your guests."

"She's pregnant. Needs to be delivered to new owners near the mountain pass on the east range. It's four hours' ride, there and back."

She frowned, not yet understanding what he meant. "Yeah?"

"Maybe it'd be nice if we took that ride together. We could leave in the morning. Back by lunchtime, if we're real quick."

Her brown eyes flickered in the light of the lanterns.

"If you go with me, though, there'll be more reason for tongues to wag."

She took a long time to answer. "Would we be safe?"

"Crawford's back in Skagway. The horse thieves are headed that way, too, otherwise Billy would've been back by now. So yes, we'd be safe. It's a well-worn trail, with scattered cabins on the way, so we wouldn't be isolated."

"It's not an overnight ride," she said, as if convincing herself.

He shook his head. "That's right."

"Then only folks who are desperate for gossip will twist it into something it's not. I'd love to spend some time with you, Harrison. It's been difficult not being able to talk freely." She lifted her pretty chin in a saucy flare of adventure, one he hadn't witnessed for days. "What time do we leave?"

"She's beautiful!" Sitting on the front porch of the doctor's house with his splinted leg propped on a sawhorse, Chuck leaned forward on the bench and cheered as Willa and Harrison led the Belgian draft horse past him for inspection.

It pleased Willa no end that Chuck's open wound hadn't festered, and that he was out this morning just past breakfast time as she and Harrison were leaving town.

The rest of the houses were quiet.

Five streets over from the tavern, the doctor's house sat on a piece of property well back from the boardwalk and the two houses on either side of it. It was a pretty parcel of land, the grass still green even though it was well into September and the fall winds were getting cool. The aspens that ringed the lot, however, were shedding their leaves.

"How far along is she?" Chuck asked.

"Three months, they figure," Willa called back. She rushed up to the porch to bid a proper goodbye to Chuck, and say good morning to the doctor himself, and his housekeeper, who were coming out the front door, no doubt because they'd heard voices.

"Thanks for taking such good care of Chuck," Harrison told them.

"My pleasure." Old Doc Leighton adjusted his cravat. Wrinkles grooved themselves into the curves around his mouth and eyes when he smiled.

"He's doing all the hard work himself." Trainee nurse Mrs. Fanny Sparks rubbed her plump hands on her apron. The cheerful woman lived right next door with her husband.

Willa and Harrison didn't stay long. They waved goodbye and rode out of town, Harrison nodding to a few of the businessmen who were opening their doors for the day.

The sun crested the mountains in a flaming red sunrise as Willa jostled gently in her saddle.

With all her years on the Montana ranch, she knew what she was doing in handling her mount.

Harrison made a striking figure of a man on horseback as he tethered the Belgian draft horse to the line behind him. The borrowed horses came from the blacksmith, too, gentle beasts that reminded Willa of home and all that had been safe and good in her life.

Wasn't it strange she had that opinion now? That thoughts of home brought a lonesome tug to her heart? She'd never anticipated how much danger and complication her trip to Alaska might entail.

However, she felt safe in the open sunshine, in having a holster of her own slung on her hip along with the gun Harrison had given her. The sun's rays beating on her shoulders gave her hope for the wonderful morning she'd spend with Harrison.

She pulled her borrowed cowboy hat low over her face to shield herself from the glare of a thousand rays, prodded her mount and rode.

They were quiet with each other for the first hour, contemplating the path ahead, not saying much more than the occasional remark about the terrain or the uplifting fall weather.

The path that led them east into the mountain valley was relatively flat and easy on the horses.

Willa inhaled the easy breeze that lifted the sleeves of her blouse and shifted across her high lacy collar. The cream color reflected the sun's heat as it began to warm up, and her hat shaded her face from sunburn. Her split skirt came in handy on the morning ride, allowing her ease of movement over the horse without the constraints of long skirts and petticoats. She wore no corset, only a tight-fitting chemise that gave her some support but let her bend in any direction she wished and didn't choke off her breathing.

Harrison let her lead on the narrow path through the woods. Ground squirrels darted around them. The bleating of mountain goats on a nearby cliff echoed between the trunks.

Shrubs of prickly rose lined a gully, its stalks four feet high, pink flowers and red rose hips standing out among the lush greens, browns and whites of the alpine fir, the white spruces and paper birch trees. What she loved most about Alaska was the scent of the air. Every few yards brought a new smell and texture—the mossy earth, the fragrant pines, the berries ripening in the slanted rays of the sun.

When the grasslands opened wide and there was enough room for two, Harrison led his mount up beside her.

"This land is remarkable." Smiling, she gazed over at his rugged face.

His cheeks were smooth from an early morning shave. Lips curled up in fine humor, brown eyes focused ahead, black Stetson tilted at an angle that gave him a dangerous appeal, the blackness accentuating the striking black eyebrows and intensity of his profile.

"You like Alaska?" he asked.

She nodded. "It would be hard to describe what it's like to live here to the people back home. Mostly what I find incredible is how the sun stays up all summer."

"Did you find it difficult to adjust when you first arrived?"

"The first day I got off that ship, I was convinced I'd never be able to fall asleep. What with the sun blazing through my hotel window at ten o'clock at night."

"What happened?"

"As soon as my head hit the pillow, I was out."

He laughed softly. "Me, too."

"How is it in the winter?"

"A lot tougher. Perpetual darkness can change a person's mood. You have to be prepared for it. Light a lot of lanterns and candles during the day. It's driven some people mad."

"Truly?"

"Oh, yeah. There was a barber in Eagle's Cliff who started attacking people with his razor."

"Did he hurt anyone?"

"Gave the banker the closest shave he'd ever had in his life. Shaved off one complete eyebrow before the guy was able to escape."

"That's awful."

"Lots of folks didn't think so. They said the banker was a money-grubber who was unfair to his customers."

"Was the barber arrested?"

"He might've been. But the next day his wife

bought two tickets back to Skagway and they left for San Francisco as soon as the ice broke."

"What happened to the mean banker?"

"He's still here, causing havoc with loans and savings. Comes into the bar occasionally."

"That guy?"

"Yup. The eyebrow eventually grew back to normal. But initially, he had to shave off his other eyebrow to be balanced. He used to comb his hair straight back, so for a time, he wound up looking like a screech owl."

Willa laughed at the picture Harrison conjured. She was still chuckling when they arrived at their destination, two cabins at the base of a mountain rimmed with mountain goats.

Her saddle creaked as she slid off her horse. Harrison introduced her to the two brothers who were awaiting their broodmare.

"She's a beaut," said the brother with short gray hair as he patted the draft horse. He barely reached the huge shoulders. The animal snorted and chewed at the grass.

The other brother, in dungarees, offered them coffee.

"We can't stay," said Harrison. "Just long enough to water our horses, but thanks just the same."

"Good luck with her." Willa patted the mare's nose.

"Watch out for the horse thieves," Harrison told

» *racines de sa volonté.* Thucydide veut connaître " les affaires des deux
» partis ", non pas pour pénétrer les secrets de l'ennemi, dénoncer les
» raisons de ses succès et mettre en évidence ses points faibles. Un tel
» désir monte-t-il à son cœur dans des moments d'impatience et de fati-
» gue? Nous ne le savons pas. Nulle part nous ne surprenons un tel
» fléchissement de sa pensée et un tel rétrécissement de son émotion. Il
» faut bien admettre chez lui, même à l'égard de Sparte, ce mouvement
» de sympathie et de curiosité sans lequel il n'y a pas d'équité. »

Ces réflexions que Jean Schlumberger écrivait en 1913, je voudrais
savoir s'il les eût écrites encore après l'été 1914 et s'il pense qu'elles
sont encore valables dans la situation d'aujourd'hui. » GIDE, *Journal,
Souvenirs,* p. 67.

13. Il ne reste de difficulté ou d'embarras que dans le *cas où
plusieurs guillemets se ferment au même endroit* du texte.

S'il est difficile d'admettre le cumul de signes [».»], on
admettra déjà plus aisément [".»].

En général, cependant, on se contente d'un seul guillemet fer-
mant, celui qui paraît le plus logique.

14. *Concurrence des guillemets avec l'italique*

Les guillemets, dans un texte, encadreront tout ce qui paraît
anormal dans la langue: un mot inconnu, un néologisme non
encore accrédité, un terme régional, technique, un mot en langue
étrangère et même un mot français auquel on donne une accep-
tion particulière, élargie ou restreinte:

Dans la voie du « péché » il n'y a que le premier pas qui coûte.
GIDE, *Journal,* p. 277.

Serais-je vraiment, comme le disent les journalistes, « inhumain »?
MONTHERLANT, *Essais,* p. 1116.

La typographie moderne préfère, en général, recourir aux
caractères italiques:

… ce café *espresso* dont vous aviez envie… BUTOR, *La Modification,*
p. 77.

Constante *vagabondance* du désir. Gɪᴅᴇ, *Journal*, p. 358.

Encore un samedi. Encore un *sabado* [sic] *de gloria*. Mᴏɴᴛʜᴇʀʟᴀɴᴛ, *Essais*, p. 806.

La concurrence peut se présenter, chez le même auteur, et, qui plus est, dans la même phrase :

S'il n'y avait que cela de « mis en cause » dans mon drame, il n'aurait pas été d'*actualité* [...]. Du reste, je vois venir un temps où les problèmes *moraux* n'intéresseront plus que quelques timorés. Gɪᴅᴇ, *Journal*, p. 1107.

15. *Pour la mention des titres d'ouvrages*, de périodiques, de journaux, on recourt aux italiques plutôt qu'aux guillemets. Dans un manuscrit, l'italique s'indique en soulignant d'un trait ce qui doit apparaître dans ce caractère.

Je viens de relire *Pot-Bouille* avec admiration. Iᴅ., *ib.*, p. 1137.

Le *Journal de Genève* relève le lugubre silence que la réponse des Alliés... Iᴅ., *ib.*, p. 614.

Afin d'éviter que se suivent deux mentions en italiques, on pourra, s'il le faut, en faire une encadrée de guillemets. Pour éviter *La Vie du langage, Le Monde* on écrirait :

« La Vie du langage », *Le Monde*.

C'est un pléonasme et une démarche inutile de cumuler guillemets et italiques. On écrira *Les Hommes de bonne volonté* et non « *Les Hommes de bonne volonté* ».

Dans certains cas, les guillemets permettront d'isoler une partie du titre général :

... la *Préface aux* « *Fleurs du Mal* » (réédition de Pelletan) dont je suis assez satisfait. Gɪᴅᴇ, *Journal*, p. 623.

V. LES VIRGULES

Les virgules, tout comme les tirets, ont leur place dans la liste des signes d'insertion. Elles marquent le fait que l'on intercale dans la phrase une proposition très courte nommée incise (*dit-il, fit-elle, s'écria-t-il, hurla-t-il, balbutia-t-il, soupira-t-elle, firent-ils en chœur*, etc.).

Le contenu des virgules d'insertion peut également être un seul mot ou un groupe de mots (*faut-il être naïf, suis-je donc bête, n'est-ce pas*, etc.).

them. "If they catch wind of your stallion and now of your broodmare, they might be tempted."

"We're well-armed, and well aware of the thieves. Thanks, kindly."

Twenty minutes later, Willa and Harrison were riding home again.

Without the broodmare, they made better time. An hour and a half later, they entered their valley.

The sun was near its noon high. She'd brought a jacket along, but it was still tied behind her saddle.

"What a refreshing way to spend the morning, Harrison."

"It's not over yet. Come take a look at this." The eagerness in his voice was infectious, and when he urged his mare around a branch off the main trail to town, she followed with a cry of excitement.

They galloped through the hills with the mountains behind them and the grasses and wildflowers blowing in the warm wind. At the top of the next crest, Harrison raced to a cluster of pine trees, dismounted, turned and waited for Willa to catch up.

Breathless, she focused on the lean cut of his dark cheeks, the shoulders that flexed beneath his shirt, the masculine way his holsters sat on his hips.

When she reached him, Harrison helped her off the saddle and she slid down his body, landing firmly at his feet and inches away from his mouth.

Chapter Fourteen

Harrison held Willa longer than necessary.

Insects buzzed in his ears, the sun shone down on his Stetson, the tall grasses by the creek hid them from any possible passersby. But there weren't any other people passing. The place was deserted except for the two of them.

She seemed to sense his buoyant mood, for she pulled her shoulders back and tilted her golden lips up at him, as if in expectation.

Sunlight streamed down the slender muscles of her throat, the pretty bones at the hollows, the lacy collar tucked so prudishly at her neck. As if a prim-and-proper blouse could save her from him, as if the split skirt that slid over her hips and slender thighs could stop him from imagining the entrancing woman beneath.

"Come," he said, taking her hand and leading her

toward the creek. The horses would be fine, grazing by the trees where they were.

"Where to?"

"I have to show you something."

"What?"

"My," he teased, "you're impatient."

She nudged him, and he was grateful for the morning with her. He led her to the top of a ridge, watching her expression when she reached the flat boulder beside him and peered down below.

Her intake of breath was audible.

"One of my favorite places." He gauged the wide expanse of grasslands below, a crescent shape that went on for acres and acres, rimmed by a ridge that followed the ocean for miles before the land met with blue water rippling in the sun.

"It's breathtaking." Willa took a step forward, perched on the very edge of the precipice, and spread her arms. "Now I know how Sir Francis Drake felt when he first saw the Cape of Good Hope."

She was standing awfully close to the rock's edge, and several weeks ago when he'd first met Willa and began to care for her, he might've snatched her back to stand on firm footing.

Don't worry so much.

The thought came to him from his dreams and he wondered for the hundredth time what it meant. Was Elizabeth trying to tell him that things would be all right with Willa?

Instead of pulling Willa back by the waistband of her skirt, Harrison took a deep breath of confidence and stepped up beside her.

The panorama made him feel like Zeus, leader of the gods and his own kingdom.

The breeze nipped at his collar, the sun blasted heat through the denim of his thighs and his eyes would surely overfill with all the vivid colors. There were turquoise waves, the white rush of the surf crashing on black boulders, purple wildflowers, dark green mosses interspersed with lighter shades of emerald.

Movement glimmered to his upper right. He turned his head, and with awe at the vision of soaring eagles, motioned to Willa. "Look."

She followed his direction and froze in wonder as three, then four, then five bald eagles, with wingspans of seven feet, patrolled the grasses below for any sign of prey.

They flew in silence, as graceful as paper kites caught on a current of air.

"That's the cliff I see every morning," she said with dawning recognition. "Lined with nests. From where the town gets its name. We're standing near the top of Eagle's Cliff."

"Mmm," he murmured, content to watch and listen. "How often do you come here?"

"As often as I can. I haven't for the past couple of weeks. There's been so much happening."

"Do you ever bump into anyone?"

"Never have."

"So the owners don't mind that you come?"

He shrugged, but the spreading smile tugging on his lips must've given him away.

"No," she breathed with amused accusation.

He raised his eyebrows in playful innocence, as if he didn't know what she meant.

She opened her mouth in astounded merriment. "You own the eagle's cliff?"

"The reason I bought here and not in Skagway. As soon as I saw it, I knew I could never leave."

Shaking her head with humor, Willa stepped back on the upper ground and tugged him backward by his sleeve.

He laughed as he caught her in his arms.

"You surprise me," he said.

Her warm brown eyes matched the color of the rich leaves. "*I* surprise *you?* How so?"

"You cover yourself up as if I can't see what's beneath."

"Is it so easy to see?"

"Not at all. The more you cover, the more I want."

A dimple of a smile tugged at her cheek. "I think it's you who—"

She didn't get any further, for he swooped down and covered her mouth with his own. She tasted perfect, and when he pulled her against his chest, her curves fell against him with all the warmth and heaven he imagined.

She wasn't wearing a corset, he'd noticed hours ago as he'd watched her breasts moving up and down gently in the saddle, and that thought sent his pulse rushing through his system. Now that she was nestled against him, he savored the natural way she felt.

Willa.

Their kiss made his mouth throb, his muscles grow into knots and his stomach tumble with the thought of being with her intimately.

When his kiss turned more dramatic, more urgent, she followed him beat for beat.

Pressing the flat palms of her hands against his chest, she slid them upward, to his shoulders, weaving her magic fingers into the back of his hair.

His reserve melted, his tempo flared. He arched over her, kissing down along the warm soft flesh of her neck, running his large hands over her slender arms, down her ribs and over the swell of her breasts.

The roundness felt right in his palms, the gentle shift of female flesh, the firmness of her breasts and the vision of how she might look, naked in the grass.

With his eager mouth still on hers, he roped his fingers into the buttons of her collar and slid one open.

She pulled back slightly, but didn't cup his hand to turn him away.

Steadily, he made his way down her blouse, unbuttoning one, then the next and the next until he'd tugged her blouse out from the waistband of her skirt to reveal a soft cotton chemise that hugged her skin. When he glanced downward, her nipples were jutting through the cloth, forming an amazing sculpture of female beauty.

He stopped at the sight.

Her face was flushed, her lips reddened from his kiss.

He hungered for her, an ache that multiplied inside his chest, an ache he needed to fill, desires he needed to satiate, heat and passion for a woman he knew better than most.

She'd only come to him a handful of weeks ago, yet he wanted to please her beyond reason. He wanted to give her sanctuary, to ease her fears about Crawford, to bring her body to the brink of lovemaking so thorough it made his head spin.

Standing in the brightness, below a poplar tree that swayed its shadows and light over her beautiful form, she gazed up at Harrison.

He couldn't see them beyond the ridge, but he could hear the horses. They were content to graze the grasses and drink from the creek.

The scent of Willa's skin and the mossy soil tingled against his nostrils, making his senses flare with life.

With steady fingers, Harrison undid the snap at her waistband and slid her skirts over her hips.

She stepped out of her clothing, tugging on intimate fabrics and stockings and stripping bare until the turn of her calf gleamed in the sunshine and her toes dug into the plush greenery.

He could stare at her forever, standing here nude except for the stretch of her chemise over the gorgeous jut of her breasts and puckering of her nipples. She seemed to have no sense of embarrassment at her lack of clothing, and he liked that very much.

He released the clasp of the pin in the back of her hair. Her long blond locks fell softly across her shoulders and curled at the cusp of her throat.

The slender muscles of her neckline against the delicate golden chain of her necklace caught a ray of light. Shade and shadow created from the tree above accentuated her beauty, the arterial hum through her flesh mimicked his own pounding rhythm beneath his ribs.

She wasn't a mirage. She wasn't something he'd imagined from days ago, wondering if he'd only dreamed of kissing her everywhere.

"You are the prettiest thing I've ever seen," he told her, unable to control himself even if he wanted. "More beautiful than the eagle's cliff."

Moments later, he was naked beside her. Still in her chemise, Willa lay sprawled in the tall fragrant grasses, her bare legs entwined with his, palming the wide expanse of his tanned chest and marveling at the shape of this god next to her. Although she'd tugged off his shirt, he had handled his own jeans.

The sun penetrated her shoulder blades through the thin cotton of her chemise and warmed her bare backside. She was too shy to take a good look at him, as much as she wanted to study his body.

"I've never made love in the sun," he said as he kissed her arm and worked his way to her shoulder.

Her stomach squeezed and rolled over with every tender bite of his mouth. Yes, she wanted this. This time, she would have him completely.

But her curiosity at his comment made her ask. "Never?"

He'd been married once, she thought. Hadn't he tried many things then?

"No," he whispered, confirming her thoughts. "Never out in the open."

The glistening of his eyes and tender lilt of his mouth told her this was something special, something unique to him as well as to her. It made her insides twist and flip all over again.

"It's never been so…" He struggled to find a word. "It's never been so natural and easy. Being together."

"I'll take that as a compliment." She kissed the lines of concern that grooved his forehead.

She wasn't naive, she hadn't expected a man like Harrison to be free of the claim of having bedded many women. Many women would want him, that was obvious within five minutes of meeting him. The draw for Willa was something much more than his devilish looks and the lucrative business he owned. It was more to do with the honest inflection of his voice and the tender tug in his throat when he spoke of intimate things.

"You know I feel the same," she whispered into his rib cage as she pressed her lips to his warm skin. "You know this is all new for me. But I don't imagine it's like this with everyone else."

"It's never been like this with *any*one else."

He stabbed her heart with his words. They came from a place pure and giving.

In response, she leaned closer, kissed his belly, smiled at the involuntary clenching of his muscles there, let her lips stray farther across the indentation of his muscled abdomen and came in full view of his shaft. Heavens, what a view. What a size. Before she allowed herself to shy away, she kissed the tip of his silky erection.

He moaned in pleasure, and she kissed her way down one side and up the satiny side of the other.

Rolling over to her knees, she positioned herself beside him. He reached out and pushed aside her chemise. He didn't let go till her breasts popped out, wedged securely by the understrapping of the cotton, jutting out into sunshine. Her areolas were warmed by the rays, and the heat felt marvelous on her bare breasts, which had never before seen the sun.

She was about to kiss him further, wondering if it would feel as good for him as it had for her when he'd pleasured her with his lips, but he quickly bent over, and so easily slid his palms under her arms and lifted her up to sit on top of him.

She gave a soft sigh of delight as she realized his target was accurate. She straddled him with her legs splayed out on either side of his hips. When she tilted her buttocks backward a little, the tip of his penis rubbed against her. There was so much pooling, such wetness whenever he caressed her. She figured it was nature's way to make it easier for making love.

He allowed her the time to do as she pleased, to slide her private parts against his, to enjoy the sensation of being together, the heat and slickness and the thick hot shaft between her legs.

But my, he was large, and she knew this would hurt.

He cupped her breasts and she stared down into his face. The shadows of blowing grasses crisscrossed the angles of his face. His jaw, once so firm against her, was softened and tilted upward.

Her gold medallion swung at her breasts, grazing his chest and glistening in the sun.

Unexpectedly, with a soft chuckle of mischief, Harrison rolled her over onto the grass so that he was perched above her, with his knees resting between hers on the grass.

There came that frown of concern, again, she noticed. "Don't stop, Harrison. I want to be with you."

"Your first time? Like this?"

"With you. I can't imagine a more lovely place. But it's you who makes it special."

He needed no more encouragement, which was good because she could barely stand to wait.

He took himself in hand and rubbed against her hot opening. The contact felt incredible, the throbbing in her muscles deepened. In a surprising move, he used his fingers to please her. The sensations felt as good as they had days ago, when he'd pleasured her with his mouth. A slow heat began to build inside of her, coaxing her to move her hips in time to his fingers, the ecstasy building and building until it washed over her, just as it had the first time with Harrison.

It was a long, deep climax, and when it finished, she was more relaxed. Gazing up with laughter inside of her, she looked to him for the next step. With a groan of complete lust, he slid inside her, slowly at first, stretching her beyond belief, then quickly.

"Breathe, honey," he whispered. He stroked her ribs and cupped her breast.

She gulped some air, trying to handle the discomfort, when just as suddenly, it started to ease.

The heat, the tight fit, the indescribable joy of being with Harrison took over. By the expression on his face, he was trying to hold back, trying to keep himself from plunging too fast.

Finally, she got a chance to study his body. The expanse of tanned muscles, the broad chest and flat stomach. The bulk of sinew and hardness and power that made up this man. A bead of perspiration appeared at his temple.

He rocked faster and deeper. Once she grew accustomed to his size, it got easier to take. When he kissed her neck, the pain faded. She wrapped her legs around his, and he must've enjoyed that, for his climax started. His shoulders stiffened, his breath caught, his thrusting became deep and measured and he moaned in pleasure.

He still had the presence of mind to kiss the tip of her breast, making her stomach do a somersault, then he lost himself in the concentration of making love to her.

Drunk with pleasure, Harrison lay against Willa in the soft grass, his arm around her, staring up at the patches of aspen leaves that fluttered above them. Turning, he pressed his head against her ribs and was captivated by the soft pounding of her heart.

"Everything about you affects me." He lifted his head and traced a lazy finger over her breastbone, out to the cliff of her velvety nipple.

She closed her eyes as he kept tracing. "That feels nice."

"The way you walk. The things you say. How you touch me."

Sighing, she rubbed the back of his head, tenderly, he thought, as a wife might do.

A wife—like Elizabeth. Harrison frowned at this unexpected train of thought. How long must he think about his former wife? How long was too long, so that he might move on, without guilt, to be with another woman?

Another flash of remorse raced through him for thinking in this manner. It wasn't that he wanted to forget Elizabeth and all they'd shared. But it seemed he'd been a boy when he was married to her. He was a different man now.

Willa's voice hummed through the sunshine. "I never thought I'd find this when I walked through your bar that day."

"I know you didn't seek this. You came to Eagle's Cliff to find some peace, and what I've done—"

"You know what I think?" She brushed away his attempt to apologize.

"Hmm?"

"Don't worry so much."

He jolted physically. Her words were Elizabeth's.

"What's wrong?" Willa bent her head forward to look at him. Her long golden hair curled around her shoulders.

His fingers stopped circling and were frozen two inches above her breast. "Nothing. I…I'm listening to what you're saying."

He tried to push his thoughts of the past from his

mind. This wasn't the place for Elizabeth. Even though he'd loved her the best he knew how, this was his time with Willa.

"Harrison?" she said after a pause.

"Yeah."

"I thought you'd drifted."

He was being selfish, thinking of himself when he had the most caring woman in the world lying next to him. "Yeah, darlin', I'm listening."

Her lashes fluttered and her mouth flexed into an awkward circle. She groped apologetically for words.

And then came the blow, as swift and silent as an unexpected gale of wind that might tear off a roof. "I don't think I'm going to stay in Eagle's Cliff."

Chapter Fifteen

Harrison sprang up beside her at the shocking words, the expanse of his bare shoulders blocking out the treetops from her view. She hesitated, trying to conquer her own fears of leaving with her need to protect him.

His dark brown eyes widened and his mouth pulsed with emotion. *"What did you say?"*

Unable to watch his reaction because she needed to express what she felt without being affected by what she thought he was thinking, she reached for her stockings and tugged them on. "I'm only thinking about it at this point. It's not for sure yet. And it's not that I don't like it here."

His voice was full of gravity, of sincerity. "Then stay."

She slid an arm into the sleeve of her blouse. Honesty would serve them both.

"And do what?" she asked softly, without accusation or judgment. "Be your bartender and hope that Crawford doesn't come back? Put you and your business at risk? Endanger your life?"

"He's a weakling who won't dare come back. I don't care about him."

"Your customers do."

She slid into her pantaloons and pulled her chemise over her head. He didn't reply immediately, but she heard the rustle of clothing beside her.

"I mean this kindly. I don't know what you get from me, Harrison. Besides the obvious."

She felt the sudden grasp of his fingers on her arm, and so swung toward him.

His jeans were on, as well as one sleeve of his shirt. His dark hair glistened in the sunlight. Roaming her face with his gaze, his demeanor was perceptive and warm, and touched her deeply. "Making love to you isn't the obvious reason why I'm here. It's a consequence of why I'm here. The extension of how I feel about you."

Leaves rippled in the noon breeze above them, their glimmering shadows falling across his chest.

"How *do* you feel about me?"

He gulped, perhaps at the turmoil in her eyes. Could he see, plain as day, that she had as much pain and conflict in her heart as there was tenderness?

He slid his warm hand down hers to reach her fingers. "That's what we're discovering, isn't it?"

Her eyes watered with a jolt of the truth. What else had she expected him to say? Was she searching for a validation for the rest of her life? Blazes, they were just getting to know each other.

He waited for an answer, but she couldn't give him one, so he kept talking, kept explaining. "I'm trying to put my past life in some perspective that makes sense."

"You mean with your late wife?"

He nodded.

"I understand, Harrison." Is that what was bothering him? What he was going through when he touched her and held her and thought about the future?

Perhaps she didn't live up to his former wife. How could she? He had married her and lived with her for years. Willa had raced into his tavern only weeks ago, with more a need for protection than love.

And that perhaps was what hurt most. Her feelings for him had grown into an overwhelming need, a desire to see him happy and prospering in life. Yet, she wasn't sure if he reciprocated with the same depth.

The realization made her take a deep breath. His feelings weren't apparent even to him. Trying to mask the unraveling of her heart, she jumped to her feet and searched for her boots.

He did the same, pulling on his pants.

The lump in her throat weighed down her words.

"You hired me as a bartender, which wasn't easy for you to do. I appreciate that and thank you."

Standing tall beside her, he angled himself closer and took her hands in his. "Don't do that. Don't put barbed wire between us."

"Let's see what happens. I'd feel a lot better about things if the deputy marshal got here for your stolen livestock."

He gripped her shoulders. "Where were you planning on going?"

Her voice held an edge of uncertainty. "Back to the lower States. Not Montana. But somewhere freer. California, maybe."

"Don't go anywhere without telling me."

She blinked up at him. After their amazing time together, not only making love, but also working elbow-to-elbow at the tavern and getting to know him like she had, she didn't want to leave him. Not now. Not ever.

"Please," he pleaded.

"All right, I promise." She would keep her word of telling him if she was leaving. *Please, Lord, don't make that necessary.*

Every hour Harrison spent with her, thought Willa as they made their way back to Eagle's Cliff, was another hour she was leading him into danger. She twisted in the saddle, trying to get comfortable. She was sore from her time with Harrison.

Crawford *was* coming back for her. He was. She felt it as sure as she knew her own name.

The butcher was a twisted man with a twisted sense of right and wrong that had nothing to do with her or Harrison.

Nothing.

But as she and Harrison rode down the ridge toward the ocean, she couldn't control how she felt at the thought of Crawford showing up again.

Sick.

Harrison, riding ahead, slowed down in the narrowing path. He ducked his tall frame beneath overhanging branches. Clouds hanging in the blue sky beyond his shoulders were lit bright orange by the sun.

He stopped unexpectedly, turned his head and lifted his face into the wind.

"What is it?"

"I thought I smelled something."

She sniffed the air several times. "All I smell is bark and grass. And salty air from the ocean."

He relaxed again in his saddle and resumed the pace.

But she was still thinking about the puzzle of Crawford.

They crossed a stream. The jostle of her saddle accentuated the soreness of her bottom. But it was easing. When the path widened, Harrison turned his wide shoulders in her direction. "We'll be home soon and you'll see. We'll be there just in time to serve the noon crowd. Crawford can't keep folks from drinking and eating, any more than he can force *himself* to stop having dinner."

She pulled back on her reins to guide her horse through a patch of rocks. "Strange you should say that. I heard him once say a similar thing, when one of his men told him business might slow down in his butcher shop. Crawford said that business will never slow down because people will never stop eating."

"Why would his business slow down?"

She froze.

It came to her in a flashing shudder. A moment of intuition so strong it was paralyzing. The hair on the back of her neck felt like razor blades. Her horse must have sensed her distress because it stopped in its tracks.

Harrison looked back again. "Willa? You all right?"

Her mind reeled with the crazy notions.

Harrison pulled back on his reins. "Willa?"

He scouted the area and reached for his gun, which made her senses snap back to her. She pressed her heels to her mare and led her horse to Harrison's side.

She gulped air as fast as she could. "Hours before Crawford came to my bedside, demanding marriage, I overheard him and his men talking. In the butcher shop, ten minutes before opening. It was eight-fifty.

The front door was unlocked so I figured the shop was open. I went in."

"What does that have to do with a forced marriage?"

"Not a forced marriage. It's what I overheard. He often had those men in the shop with him. They got to know each other on the ships on their voyage to Alaska, Crawford had once told me. I always thought some of his friends looked rough and questionable, but I gave him credit for having so *many* friends. For building up a business from nothing."

"What did you overhear that's so strange?"

"I chalked it up to an innocent business discussion. They were planning to meet that night at someone's stables. An odd hour, now that I think about it. Talking about cattle, and something about how his sales had dropped. How difficult it was to find livestock unaccounted for."

"Unaccounted for? Those were his exact words?"

"Yes."

"But he buys his meat at auction, I imagine. All accounted for."

"And he orders some livestock directly from Oregon. By ship. Also accounted for, tallied by the head as well as the pound."

"Then what is *unaccounted* for?" Harrison leaned onto his saddle horn.

They both came to the conclusion at the same time, but Willa said it first. "Any livestock he can steal. They talked about the black market. In meats. How the prices kept going up and up. But Crawford didn't say it with any sign of disgust, like an honest butcher would."

Harrison sucked in a lungful of air. "He was pleased. Happy to see the prices soar because he controls the goddamn black market."

"It fits." Her voice could barely keep up to her rapid thoughts. "As the town butcher, he's in a position to accept any amount of livestock he can handle. Wagonloads are often delivered way past closing time. Once I saw the wagons at midnight. I was returning to the boardinghouse after a night of dancing with my friends."

"Hell," Harrison muttered. "Right underneath our noses. Deputy marshal's, too."

Willa stiffened with a new thought.

"What is it?" he asked.

"That's why he wanted to marry me. To shut me up. He was nervous that morning. Jumped nearly two feet off the ground when I bid him hello unexpectedly. Strange looks darted between him and his friends."

"And when you refused to marry him, he had to come after you."

"I'm not sure if he wants to marry me or kill me."

"That son of a bitch," Harrison said, seething. He rubbed his bristly jaw and adjusted his posture in the saddle. "He's behind it all. My stables. Chuck's broken leg."

Willa twisted her mouth in revulsion. "He's got a perfect cover as a butcher. No one suspects him."

"Except maybe the law in Skagway."

Harrison turned his mare around to face the direction of home and they urged their horses to ride faster.

Willa pressed her heels to her mare. "Why the deputy marshal?"

"When I sent word for Quinn, I gave him a message for Jackson. Indicating the problems you were having with Crawford."

She couldn't have heard him right. "Pardon me?"

He broke into a gallop and she strained forward to keep up. Her skirts flew and her blouse billowed in the wind.

"Your problems with Crawford! I asked Deputy Marshal Jackson to check him out!"

Burning with a sudden flash of anger, Willa pulled back hard on her reins. Her horse responded and came to an abrupt stop.

Harrison doubled back to her side. "What is it?"

She tried to keep the accusations out of her tone, but her voice remained rigid, her lips tight. "Tell me I misunderstood. You did *not* disclose the very thing I asked you not to tell."

"Crawford's a menace. You need protection."

"You sent word to the lawman without asking my permission? Without warning me?"

Harrison grappled for words. "I'm trying to protect you, Willa, not harm you."

"Don't you see?" she snapped. "Crawford found out. He intercepted your message. That's how he knew to come looking for me *here*."

"No," Harrison replied, "that can't be true. How would he intercept any message? I trust Zeb with my life. It was in a sealed envelope and Zeb would never have opened it."

"Maybe it was stolen."

Harrison shook his head. "Couldn't have been. It *got* to my brother because Quinn replied."

"Then Crawford heard it from one of your brother's men. Or from the lawman himself. I don't know how, but it happened!"

Shaken and trembling, she repositioned herself in the saddle. Leather creaked beneath her thighs.

Birds chirped in the shrubs around them, bobbing and fluttering with cheerful energy, such a contrast to how disappointed she was feeling in Harrison.

He turned his face away from her, pulling the brim of his hat down low to shade his eyes from the sun's glare, but likely to shade his tight expression from her. His jaw tensed. He held his head high, gazing out across the vast expanse of the valley.

With a click of his tongue, he urged his mare along, and they set off for the town again, both likely contemplating what exactly they were going to do about Crawford. And she still disbelieving that Harrison could've broken her confidence like this.

When they turned the final bend of the pathway

before the main trail appeared to the outskirts of town, she watched Harrison rear up in his saddle.

He leaned into the wind, hips rigid, legs straight in his stirrups.

"Oh, no," he breathed.

She whipped her head to the direction he was facing. The town's buildings sat clustered on the edge of the ocean. Two ships were sailing on the water.

Was that a curl of smoke?

Something wasn't right.

"I *did* smell it," he said, almost to himself, as if she weren't there.

"Smoke," she confirmed. Her legs tensed, her vision sharpened.

"Where's it coming from? East or west side? It can't be. Not my livery stables."

With a loud shout, Harrison flicked his reins and tore off. His Stetson caught in the wind and ripped from his head, but he kept going.

Her heart thundered against her ribs as she gave chase.

A plume of smoke billowed high across the grasslands, above the town of Eagle's Cliff. The smoke had doubled in size from moments ago. What building was on fire? Was anyone hurt?

Chapter Sixteen

Harrison and Willa galloped full force toward the catastrophe a mile away.

The wind kicked at his skin and whizzed through his hair. The sound of hooves hammered against the beaten trail. Beneath his thighs, the muscles of the mare strained and released, strained and released, in rhythm to Harrison's panting breath.

The butcher was behind it, Harrison thought with every pounding cell of his body. He cursed the day the man set foot on Alaskan soil.

Harrison urged his mare to breakneck speed, thinking Willa might fall behind, but with her riding skills, she was right beside him. The breeze snatched her hair and threw it behind her shoulders, her sleeves sailed through the wind, her thighs pressed tight against her mare. She had full command of her animal.

As they drew closer to the town and were able to see more, they reined in their horses.

"It's not my property." Harrison rubbed his forehead in a mixture of confusion. "My buildings are fine." Anxiety for his neighbors weighed upon him.

He narrowed his eyes over the rows of plank and log buildings, trying to discern why the smoke was coming from deeper within the town.

Could he be wrong about Crawford? Maybe he wasn't the cause of the fire. Maybe the fire had started from a woodstove, or a flickering candle, or someone careless with a lantern.

If Crawford *had* done it, he would've lit Harrison's property sky high. Harrison knew it, sure as hell, because he had the most precious thing Crawford wanted in this world.

Willa. His safety net in this criminal game he was playing. Taking her as his wife so she couldn't testify against him, controlling her with violence, or perhaps wanting to snuff out her voice completely. Why he hadn't already ended her life wasn't hard to figure out. The beast wanted her in his bed first.

"What building is it?" Willa shifted in her saddle and peered into the stream of smoke. She coughed and rubbed her face.

"Take it easy, now." Harrison brought his mare to a trot. "Let's swing around this way, out of the wind."

They took the fork in the path that led them toward the western side of town. As the buildings grew bigger, Harrison made out the shapes of dozens of people running toward the fire. Some had already set up a bucket line toward the ocean. Others were wheeling wagons loaded with barrels of freshwater they had stored for their livestock.

The shouting was a pitch of voices, some hollering directions, others calling friends' names.

When Harrison and Willa turned onto the final rutted street and discovered the burning building with its painted blue porch, he groaned in recognition.

"The doctor's house."

"Chuck." Willa flew off her horse and searched the dozens of faces.

Harrison put the horses in a safe alcove, four houses down from the fire, and raced to catch up.

They found Chuck lying on the grass, propped up beside a wagon with the old doctor trying to make him drink from a ladle of water. Chuck's broken femur was splinted with two large pegs down either side of his leg from thigh to ankle, and wrapped completely with bandages.

The young man had his eyes closed and was unresponsive. His face was almost as pale as the bandages wrapped around his leg. With alarm, Harrison discreetly slid his fingers over Chuck's wrist, feeling for a pulse.

The hand was stone cold. Frantic, Harrison kept searching.

There. There it was. A weak beat.

He felt a storm of gratitude, quickly followed by rage welling up inside his chest at who might do this.

"I tried," the old doctor coughed. His usually well-groomed white hair was covered in soot, falling forward across his temples in disarray. "I tried to get him out sooner." Another cough. "But…but my housekeeper fell down. She was unconscious and I had to drag her out." He rubbed his bleary eyes. "Not as strong as I used to be."

"Shhh," said Willa, placing a comforting hand on his soot-stained shoulders. "Thank goodness you got them both out." The old guy collapsed to his knees. She dived to help him.

"Blankets," Harrison hollered to the people scurrying behind him. "We need blankets over here!" He jumped up and found some on the wagon behind him.

Hacking overtook the old man. Harrison took a good look at him and realized the doctor was in dire distress. His eyes were sunken, lips turning blue.

"Lawrence, I've known you awhile now, and you should rest. You're not breathing too easy."

Coughing seized him. He wheezed, gasping for air. Harrison led him gently to the other side of the wagon to sit beside Chuck, who was still unconscious.

"My…" The doctor tried to explain, but his hacking made his voice weak. "Fanny…" he called after his housekeeper.

"I'll find Fanny and take a look at her, Lawrence, you stay here and rest."

"I want to…to go…" He kept coughing, his face turning redder and redder. His cheeks puffed out like one of those small ocean creatures. Then, giving Harrison a fright, the old man's lips and face turned completely blue.

The doctor keeled over. Unconscious.

Willa snatched at the man's collar, loosening his tie and the buttons to give him room to breathe while Harrison lifted him to the soft grass.

Harrison threw a blanket over Dr. Leighton and another over Chuck. He grabbed hold of the doctor's wrist and searched for a pulse. Nothing. Harrison scrambled to find one at his throat. Nothing. He tried again and again, then shook the old shoulders.

No response.

Harrison tilted him, gave him a hard thump between the shoulder blades, shook him some more, shouted in his ears, but nothing worked.

There was no life left in him.

Willa, going through grief of her own, helped Harrison call the doctor's name. "Lawrence. Lawrence. Dr. Leighton, *please*."

Finally, after many minutes of trying to bring the old guy back, Harrison slumped back on his knees.

His voice trembled with all the emotions he was feeling—despair, heartache and outrage. "I think his heart gave out."

Crouched beside the fallen doctor, Willa let out a sob.

The tempo of Harrison's breathing grew in his ears. Fury choked his words. "Crawford's sending me a message that I can't save my friends. He did this."

"Harrison!" a stranger—a man—called in the distance.

Willa heard it ten minutes after the doctor had passed away, but didn't recognize the voice. She and Harrison attended to the doctor's housekeeper, Mrs. Fanny Sparks, at the buggy where she was recuperating. Her husband, a local fisherman, fussed over her. Willa was more concerned with the housekeeper than who might be calling Harrison.

She patted the arms of the elderly woman, who was encased in a shawl. "Are you breathing better, Fanny?"

"Better," she rasped. "I can't believe the doctor is gone."

"He wouldn't want you to suffer over him," Harrison told her gently. "He'd want you to do everything in your power to regain your strength."

Fanny settled into the seat of the buggy and her husband eased in next to her. Several of the other townswomen came to check on her, including Lily McCloud, who brought water to drink and biscuits to nibble on for the folks fighting the fire and those caught unexpectedly by the smoke who needed to rest.

"Harrison!" the stranger shouted again.

Harrison wheeled around from the buggy and a look of hope sprung to his face. "Quinn!"

Willa turned and witnessed a dark-haired man in a fringe suede jacket leap off his horse. He was armed with a holster and guns.

He shook Harrison's hand and smacked him on the shoulder. "You all right?"

"Yeah." Harrison stepped back, and the man Willa understood to be his brother surveyed the fire.

Two other armed riders followed him on horseback, one wearing a badge. The deputy marshal. Following right behind were Billy and Michael.

Help had finally arrived.

Quinn shook his head at the burning building, which thankfully hadn't spread to the surrounding structures. It was set back on its own slice of land, twenty yards away from neighboring houses. "Hell, what happened here?"

Harrison ignored the question for a moment. "You got my note."

"Yeah. Sorry the court case took so long." The tall dark stranger peered over at Willa and it was then she noted the remarkable resemblance between the men. Dark hair, lean-muscled bodies, thick through the shoulders.

Brothers in every sense.

Harrison nodded toward her politely. "This here is Willa." He didn't offer the surname of Banks or Somerset, and she felt relieved they weren't getting into that right now.

Apparently, Quinn Rowlan didn't need a surname

to peg who she was. In a businesslike fashion, he leaned over quickly to shake her hand, too. "Pleased to meet you. Sorry 'bout the troubles you're going through."

"Thank you."

He turned back to Harrison. "What can you tell me?"

"Crawford's men are responsible for this. Maybe he's even in these parts himself. Someone saw him leaving on a ship to Skagway, but maybe the ship stopped soon after it left and he got off. I doubt he lit the fire himself, coward that he is." Harrison took a long deep breath in the direction of the fallen man who'd been placed in the back of the wagon. "Unfortunately, the doctor's dead."

Quinn's face twisted in sympathy. "Crawford won't get away with murder, Harrison. I can promise you that."

Willa, still sorrowful for the doctor's passing, was grateful to have Quinn here. The two muscled brothers standing together seemed invincible.

Quinn scuffed the dirt with his boot. "Why this house?"

"He must've known Chuck was here. Everyone up and down the coast knows Doc Leighton's house, with its blue porch. Maybe the plan was to finish Chuck off. To send me a message not to interfere with what Crawford's after." Harrison's gaze shifted to her subtly, indicating to Quinn that she was the prize.

She lowered her head in shame and anger.

"Miss, it's not your fault." Quinn's big cowboy boots turned toward her until she looked back up at him. "In my days as district attorney, I've seen an awful lot of crazy people. This man's mad and it's got nothing to do with you."

Willa decided she liked Harrison's brother. She liked them both. And maybe her anger at Harrison for disclosing her whereabouts to Deputy Marshal Langford, and her situation with the butcher, was something she should forgive.

"You won't do anything reckless, yourself, will you?" Quinn continued.

She understood what he was saying. The same thing Harrison had been telling her. That running away from the situation, that being frightened into fleeing, was maybe what Crawford was after. And that it wouldn't accomplish anything. She wouldn't be any safer, and Harrison likely wouldn't be, either.

"I won't," she said firmly. She looked to Harrison, whose hard expression softened around the edges of his eyes and mouth, as though he finally believed her.

"Excuse us for a moment," Harrison told her. "I've got to speak to Jackson. And catch up with Billy."

She nodded. "Go ahead. I'll…I'll stay with Fanny and her husband."

An hour passed as Willa helped the dozens of

firefighters and the women who supported them. The men continued pumping water and throwing buckets. The fire began to subside, in truth likely because the house had been completely engulfed and there was nothing more to burn, but everyone breathed a sigh of relief that no other buildings had succumbed.

Two hours later, the house was a pile of red embers, logs still flickering in the center, and still much too hot to approach.

The casket maker had ordered the doctor's body to be removed, and a funeral was set for tomorrow at the church.

Harrison was still deep in talks with Quinn and the lawman. They focused on a piece of paper spread out on the back of a wagon, pointing and drawing lines on what seemed to be a makeshift map.

It was evening when the fire was finally out and the last of the men could leave.

She joined the group that settled into the tavern, where Harrison and his brother and the lawmen continued their talks around a table.

After washing up and a quick change in her room, Willa came to join them in the tavern as George and Natalie served them rabbit stew and greens.

Harrison pulled up a chair for her, between himself and his brother. She felt odd, like an interloper almost. Harrison must've sensed it, for he planted a warm hand on her shoulder. The gesture was comforting and perhaps what she needed after such a frightening day.

"You coming with us, Harrison?" Deputy Marshal Langford removed his hat and planted it on the table. His gray vest covered his tall torso, but hung off his thin chest.

Willa surmised they were talking about going after Crawford and his men.

Harrison rubbed her shoulder blade. "I'm not about to leave Willa by herself."

She didn't argue this time. She trusted Harrison's judgment.

"I can leave one of my deputies behind with her. No one can track a man like you can." Jackson planted his elbows on the table, lifting a forkful of meat to his mouth as he explained to Willa. "I don't know how much you know about Harrison, but the three of us here were all wrongly accused of crimes we didn't commit. Spent two years together on the trails, searching for the men who framed us."

"You found them." Willa raised a biscuit to her lips. "You cleared your names."

Jackson nodded.

Quinn lowered his water glass to the table. "Ah, so you do know the story." He looked to Harrison and some sort of signal passed between them she didn't understand. Like a signal of encouragement, as two brothers might do.

Jackson pointed his fork at Harrison and stabbed

the air for emphasis. "Will you come take a look at the tracks? Maybe there's something you'll see that my men haven't caught yet."

"Quinn and I both agree the fire was set from the back," said Harrison. "They rode in on two horses and threw a lit rag into the pile of wood that was stacked against the back wall of the house. Prints are still in the ground, and eyewitnesses describe two men fleeing on horseback."

"Yeah," said Jackson. "The tracks lead to the ridge. Where those eagles nest. You know the one I mean?"

Willa lowered her head to focus on her plate, but a tide of heat flushed up her face. She knew very well the ridge he meant. The place where she and Harrison had made love. Her troubles then had been smaller. Now, there was an innocent man dead. Poor Doc Leighton.

"Yes," said Harrison, and other heads nodded. "Of course. Where the eagles fly."

Beneath the table, Harrison touched her thigh.

The deputy marshal continued explaining. "I've got two men on their trail right now and the rest of us will join them after our discussion." He soaked up the gravy from his plate with the last of his bread and turned to Harrison one more time.

"We wouldn't leave this young lady unattended, Harrison, you know that. Dylan here, my deputy, and several of the men in town could haul themselves up in your tavern, right here, protecting her."

The corner of Harrison's mouth twisted upward. He wanted to go. She could see it in his concentration, the hesitation to say no.

"You should go if you'd be of help," Willa urged him, with all eyes suddenly on her. Lantern lights flickered above them, glistening off their drinking glasses and cutlery. "Seems a waste of a good man to sit cooped up in the tavern with me. They need you."

Chapter Seventeen

Harrison leaned forward with his elbows on the table, and said what he knew to be right. What he'd always believe to be right.

"I stand by Willa."

"Fair enough." Quinn nodded and the rest of the men knew not to push Harrison further.

He didn't look over at Willa because she was likely displeased. But he wasn't about to go chasing after Crawford at the expense of her safety.

Crawford be damned. He'd get his own just reward.

Quinn and Jackson would have to do the finding and hauling back to jail in Skagway. Harrison had already discussed with them the incriminating conversation Willa had overheard in the butcher shop. Combined with a few details Jackson had picked up in Skagway about the butcher, there was enough to arrest him.

Billy hadn't been able to ascertain the whereabouts of Harrison's stolen livestock. The thieves must've slipped in and out of the two harbors by ship, sight unseen.

As for Chuck, Fanny and her husband had insisted on taking him into their home for the recovery period. Chuck had been agreeable and appreciative.

"Thanks kindly for the meals, Harrison." Jackson rose, nodded to George and Natalie, who were slower than usual serving food due to the fire they'd also helped extinguish that afternoon. In fact, the whole tavern had cleared of people when the fire had struck, including Sarah and Rosa. Everyone had rushed to help the doctor, and Harrison was grateful for the kindness of good neighbors.

A few dinner guests entered the front doors as Jackson and his men were squeezing past on their way out.

"Good luck to you all," said Willa, rising and shaking hands with Quinn. "Your help is much appreciated."

"It's our pleasure and our duty, miss," Quinn replied.

Things were beginning to return to normal in the tavern. Shamus checked the registrar of guests as a newcomer sauntered in with miner's hat in hand, carrying a gun belt like the rest of them, but with shovel and pickax strapped to his bag.

"You got the last room, but you can leave your mining equipment at the livery stables," Shamus told him.

"If you don't mind, I hear there's been some thievery lately. Feel safer with it all under my watchful eye."

"Suit yourself," said Shamus, showing him up the stairs.

Willa got back to work behind the bar, but Harrison walked his brother outside. "How's your wife? How's Autumn?"

Quinn adjusted the brim of his Stetson in the cooling light of the evening. "Sends her regards. She's singing up a storm and saving every penny of her wages for a hotel of her own one day."

The words were heavier on Harrison than he was used to feeling when Quinn spoke about his wife. Perhaps it was because Quinn seemed so satisfied with his life with Autumn. Marriage, for Quinn, hadn't been near as unsettling as another marriage for Harrison might be. Or maybe it wouldn't. His feelings for Willa were growing unstoppable.

But that was another matter for another time.

Harrison said his goodbyes and wished the men well in their search for Crawford. "I'll be waiting for your message, like we agreed. If you need anything, more supplies, anything, just send word."

With a warm handshake to his brother, Harrison turned and reentered the tavern. He slid in behind the bar with Willa, working quietly by her side for the next six hours.

They stopped only long enough to take a break when they were thirsty and hungry, otherwise he enjoyed her proximity and the warm comfort of her presence.

Her skirts rustled around her high-heeled boots. Her blouse stretched around her bosom and fit snugly against the curve of her back as she poured ales and beers. The mirrored glass on the wall behind them, however, reflected the low volume of customers, a fact that didn't escape Harrison, and one he knew was nagging at her, too.

There was no privacy between them to talk about their day, the intimacy they'd shared high atop the ridge, the resulting argument of his disclosing her whereabouts and problems to the deputy marshal and most of all, the growing feelings for her that Harrison was so desperately trying to stifle, at the same time trying to articulate to Willa.

Elizabeth came to him in his dreams, dressed in the pretty green gown she'd often worn to church. Except the buttons were different, Harrison noticed, more shiny, and there was a flimsy gauze fabric on top of everything that made her look wispy and not of this world.

Her flesh felt real, however, as she kissed his cheek. It was warm and fragrant as it always was.

"Goodbye," she said gently in the spring sun-shine, as he sat on a boulder behind their barn in North Dakota, watching her walk toward him. "You won't be needing me anymore."

"What do you mean?" He tugged at her warm hand. "I'll always need you."

"I have loved ones to see. My mother's here."

Even in his dream, Harrison knew something wasn't right. Her mother had long passed. Where was she? Where was here?

"And my pa." Elizabeth ran her hand over the fine fabrics of her gown. "He'd like to take me fish-ing. You know how squeamish I am. He promised to set the hook for me." Her face lit up.

It wasn't right. She hated fishing.

She might fall in the water, Harrison thought, rising with concern, opening his mouth to try to warn her from straying to the river's edge. No words came out. He struggled to open wider, but his throat wouldn't cooperate, wouldn't release any communi-cation.

She walked away as quietly and beautifully as she'd come. He struggled to scream now, how terri-fied he was for her safety. She stopped, turned back and, with a tender look over her shoulder, blew him a kiss.

"You know how I feel about you. How I'll always feel about you," she whispered. "But it's time you go."

He couldn't move. Couldn't breathe. A butterfly fluttered past. A breeze lifted the sweat from his brow, but the heaviness remained on his chest.

Looking down at his hands, he rotated them in the air, marveling at the odd sheen of dotted sprinkles that gleamed in the sunlight as though they were remnants of gold dust. He looked up again and she was gone.

He flew to his feet. *Not like this.* He had to tell her one last thing. He ran and ran and ran, out of breath and panting in the cold. Somehow it was winter now and the snow drifts were knee deep, but he couldn't catch up to the woman in his dreams.

The following morning, hit with a strange sense of melancholy although he couldn't quite remember what he'd dreamed, Harrison dressed for the funeral of his good friend, Doc Leighton.

Lawrence had no relatives anyone knew of. His closest friends had been his housekeeper Fanny and her husband, so they were the ones who made the decisions for the chapel services today.

Harrison was to be a pallbearer, along with Bruce Sparks, Fanny's husband, and four other businessmen in town the doc had favored as friends.

Dressed in his best blue jeans and newly polished cowboy boots, Harrison went downstairs in the early morning light.

He stoked the fires to heat the place from the drop in overnight temperatures.

Out of respect for the doctor, he turned the sign in the tavern's window to Closed.

No one else was up yet. The guests upstairs were still sleeping. Last night, Harrison had told all his staff they had the day off for the funeral. George and Natalie had ensured there was plenty of food in the kitchen for guests to help themselves during this unusual time.

Shamus and Billy, however, were stationed in the bunkhouse and keeping their eyes open for any signs of potential trouble from Crawford or his men, if they chose to show their grimy faces.

Footsteps tapped lightly on the stairs behind Harrison, and he turned around to witness Willa coming down to join him.

"Willa Somerset, you are a sight to behold." Harrison bowed his head in admiration. Her presence instantly made this day seem much more hopeful and alive.

She smiled shyly, as if wondering if it was all right to smile on a day like today. Taking the last step, she lifted a fistful of skirts and petticoats. The rustle of lace and the sight of her high-heeled boots strapped with a multitude of buttons drew his gaze. The same ones she'd worn on the day he'd met her, the same ones he still found seductive.

Reaching the plank floor, she squeezed around the empty tables and came toward him like a warm summer breeze. Her blouse was the color of apricots, a shade deeper than her strands of lustrous gold hair. She'd tied part of it behind her head in a big black bow. Most of it curled forward around her neck and clung against the soft curve of her breasts. The blouse was one he hadn't seen before, lacy on the front and pinched as it gathered in the waist to tuck into her long black skirt.

"I don't have an appropriate black blouse," she said, glancing down at her sleeves. "Maybe I should borrow—"

"You look just right. Doc Leighton would say so himself. Everyone knows you're too young to have a lot of black in your wardrobe."

This seemed to set her at ease. Her shoulders slackened and her smile deepened. Her smooth skin glowed with a healthy sheen.

He took her hand and drew her to the windows. Standing there quietly, they gazed out at the awakening street.

It was cloudy and gray. Across the boardwalk in a building on the other side, the tinsmith's light was on. Beside him, the jeweler was sweeping his front stoop. Two women walked by with baskets in hand, filled with wildflowers, and Harrison guessed they were headed to the chapel to decorate.

Harrison trailed his arm around Willa's shoulders, enjoying the heat that seeped into his fingers. "We never had a chance to talk about yesterday."

"So much happened."

He didn't want her to suffer over the tragic course of events, and silently cursed Crawford. "Did you get any sleep?"

"I'm embarrassed to say I slept quite well."

"I'm glad. You were exhausted. It's important to go on for the sake of those who left us. And for the strength to fight those who want to defeat us."

"Did you get any rest?"

"Some." Save for a restless dream he couldn't recall.

A shuffling of boots on the upper landing jarred them both out of the conversation and made him realize they weren't alone.

Harrison and Willa turned their heads upward, but no one appeared. The sounds were coming from the direction of the men's room.

"We keep getting interrupted." Harrison turned back to Willa. "Sorry. There's more we need to discuss." About their hour on the ridge, he thought, hoping she'd understand he wanted to talk more about the questions she'd asked him. About his feelings toward her, about the mistakes he was making and his fear of losing her.

Another door upstairs creaked. It was getting busy. Harrison turned to look just in time to see the door next to her room snap shut. Then the men's room opened and the tall miner who'd checked in yesterday came out, yawned, tucked his shirt past his holsters and went back into his room.

Standing here talking to Willa about such intimate things was dangerous to her reputation. Harrison had no right to say it in front of an audience.

"Let's find some time alone this afternoon to talk. After the services."

She nodded, moistening her lips and weaving her fingers together. "I'd like that, Harrison." Her gentle words gave him unexpected strength.

When he looked outside again, a light rain bounced against the boardwalk and beaded in the ruts of the street. A flicker of disappointment bristled against his skin. Not the best circumstances for a burial.

There was much Willa had to say to Harrison, too, she thought as she battled the rain to enter the little church nestled far below the base of the eagle's cliff.

Rain pelted the colorful stained-glass windows. The air smelled musty, a combination of lit candles and incense. Willa found a seat beside Lily, who was dressed spectacularly in a wide black hat and smart black suit that looked feminine, yet appropriately modest for the occasion.

Willa nodded and slipped her shoulders out of the drenched oil slicker Harrison had lent her. He was seated in the front pew along with the other pallbearers. The plain pine casket sat in front of the altar.

To the other side, Fanny and her husband sat with Chuck, who they'd wheeled into the church in a well-worn wheelchair, his broken leg propped up. Bless them for having found the contraption in such a faraway place in the world.

"Morning," Lily whispered.

"Howdy," Willa murmured to her friend.

Heads turned toward them, including the baker's wife, Mrs. Whittler, and her daughter, Morgan, seated farther along the pew, neither of whom showed any distaste for Willa this morning. Perhaps they'd leave their quarrels behind, feeling as Willa did that the death of the town doctor put other minor grievances into better perspective.

Such as her own with Harrison. Their arguments from yesterday seemed almost pointless today. She'd been so fearful when she'd discovered he'd told the deputy marshal who she was and that Crawford was after her, that she'd barely absorbed Harrison's explanations, let alone accepted them for what they were. Acts of concern for her well-being.

Her fear of Crawford wasn't completely erased, but now that the lawman, his men and Quinn were after the criminal, there was no sense worrying herself to death. And it was touching that Harrison had decided to stay with her at the hotel.

When the choir struck the first note of "Amazing Grace," a feeling of gratitude sprang up inside of her and Willa sang with the rest of them.

It was a beautiful ceremony, with Harrison giving the eulogy and surprising her with how well he knew the doctor—apparently they'd arrived in Alaska on a ship together, meeting each other for the first time two years ago, but they hadn't met up again till earlier this year.

Most of all, she was surprised by the warmth Harrison generated among his friends here in the cozy chapel, with its cast-iron stove spitting out heat and the water coming in torrents down the panes. He had a presence and a charm that enthralled her as she watched the color of the misty morning light wash over his dark cheeks and glimmer against the black folds of his suit jacket.

The reverend ended his sermon on a note of caution. In black robes with a string tie and white shirt, thick gray hair parted in the center, he closed his Bible and turned to the pouring rain on the patches of red and green and blue stained glass.

"Maybe we should hold off on the burial till the rain stops some."

The pallbearers rose to stand around the casket, such a poignant picture of six handsome men showing such respect for a fallen friend.

The congregation rose to their feet. Murmurings, sounds of boots shuffling and hymnals being slid to the backs of pews filled the air for a few seconds till there was silence again.

Harrison, facing the crowd, looked toward Willa

and she wondered what he was thinking, and how they might work through their problems.

"Reverend," said Harrison, "what if the men stay behind to lay the good doctor to rest, but the women go ahead to prepare for the reception? Some of the ladies are already drenched and cold."

"Good idea," other men murmured.

"Let it be," said the reverend. Then he rubbed his forehead as if he had a headache. Was he feeling all right? Someone else tapped his elbow and he murmured that he was fine.

A big meal was planned at the baker's home, but Willa wasn't sure if she was invited, seeing how the baker's wife didn't readily approve of her. Of course Willa knew everyone was *probably* invited, but she wasn't sure if she was *welcome*.

When the congregation dispersed and people made their way down the aisles, Mrs. Whittler placed a hand on Willa's shoulder as she passed.

It wasn't a big gesture, in fact, unnoticeable by most other folks, but the light pressure on Willa's shoulder blade told her she was indeed a part of the town.

She nodded kindly to the baker's wife, and turned around to find Harrison before she left. He was deep in discussion with the reverend, though, and didn't see her.

On her way out into the storm, Willa draped her oil slicker over her shoulders and spoke to Lily. "Harrison wanted to deliver some wine to the meal. Shamus and

Billy are guarding the tavern. I'll ask Billy to help me bring it over, since Harrison's held up."

"Don't be late," said Lily. "Not because of the wine—we'll wait to eat till all the men get there—but because we'll miss your company."

It was another friendly gesture and Willa was buoyant as the others walked her to the tavern, then said goodbye.

Shamus and Billy greeted her in the kitchen, guns holstered to their hips. "It's all quiet. Some of the guests left to go about their business. Some are staying put due to the weather."

Willa saw to the packed crate of wine Harrison had indicated last night, saying hello to the four guests playing cards in the bar as she passed.

Shamus and Billy took the crate out to the livery stables to haul it over by horse and buggy, since they had to go some distance and it would be difficult to carry by hand. Willa headed to the spring room to wash her hands and tidy her wet hair, then she'd meet them outside.

Humming one of the hymns she'd heard this morning, she thought of the afternoon ahead. Perhaps she'd spend some time with Mrs. Whittler and explain what had happened with Crawford and why she had to keep her identity a secret when she first arrived. Perhaps business in the tavern might pick up if the older women of the town got to know her.

Willa slipped inside the door of the private spring

room and turned to secure the shiny new latch Harrison had installed. She stopped in horror.

Crawford stood behind the door, as big as a horse, leering at her and pointing his gun right between her eyes.

Chapter Eighteen

Harrison wondered where she was.

Willa hadn't arrived yet, although it was well after one o'clock when Harrison and the pallbearers stepped through the front door of Festus Whittler's home. More than an hour after Harrison had last seen her. The place was five streets over from the tavern, attached to the bakery shop and café from where the aromas of fresh-baked strudel and scones saturated the damp air.

Thunder cracked down on the roof. Harrison and his friends had worked quickly in the downpour to bury Doc Leighton and say their last respects.

"Where's Reverend Thomas?" Heavyset Mrs. Whittler shuffled the men through the door and closed it to the pounding water. They removed their oil slickers, and she led them to the spring room where they could wash up.

"He'll be along shortly," Harrison told her,

drying his fingers on a soft towel and following her back out the door. "Wanted to change into his street clothes, he said."

Harrison scoured the parlor as well as the people seated and talking by the fireplace.

No Willa.

He followed his friends into the kitchen, then the bakery and seating area of the café.

No Willa.

A crack of lightning lit the bakery window red. After the initial gasp, folks in the room giggled in the nervous tension.

Festus, looking neater and cleaner than he usually did while seated at Harrison's bar, took a swig of coffee. "I dare say the doctor would be the first to laugh at the mad storm and the timing of it all."

Harrison agreed, wondering where Willa was.

Had she decided to stay home? Surely she'd know that folks wanted her here. That *he* wanted her here.

"Shall we set out the food?" Mrs. Whittler addressed the ladies.

They murmured positive responses. Lily Mc-Cloud was the first to step up and remove a tea towel from a bowl of mixed greens.

Harrison wasn't about to eat without Willa.

Maybe he ought to go to the tavern and see where she and Billy were. Harrison trusted his men to protect her and knew that Quinn and the deputy marshal would corner Crawford in the mountains.

Maybe Billy was the holdup. Maybe he and Shamus were switching places in watching over her, and Shamus would be leading her here, along with the crate of wines Harrison had packed.

Or maybe she'd changed her mind about Harrison and didn't want anything more to do with him.

The thought hit him like a slug to the chest.

Earlier this morning, he'd suggested they take some time to talk this afternoon. Maybe she'd rolled it around in her head and decided since he wasn't able to voice how he felt about her yesterday, she was backing off completely.

Could he blame her?

How exactly did he feel? Why was he stuck in this—

"Have some," Festus shouted, shoving a sugar-coated pastry into Harrison's hands and interrupting his train of thought.

The sweet was still warm from the ovens and crackling with ground bits of white sugar. While the men around him joked and complained about the weather, Harrison stared at his hands.

The pastry left its mark on his skin, and suddenly his dream of the night before came roaring back to life. Like the gold dust from his sleeping vision, the bits of sugar glistened on his palms. He lifted one hand and rotated his fingers, mesmerized by the dancing light just as he'd been last night. He remembered his frantic search for Elizabeth, trying to tell her one last thing before she disappeared forever.

He gazed with hope and pain at the sugar. It was her. Elizabeth was back to give him the opportunity to say what he needed.

"I'm sorry," he whispered. *Sorry for the morning when you died. It should've been me letting out the horses. It should've been me.*

"Here," Mrs. Whittler said, shoving a checkered napkin into his hand, interrupting his view of the sugar.

Was he going mad?

He didn't think so. He'd had an opportunity to say what he'd been feeling for all these years, the apology he'd never been able to give Elizabeth even in his dreams.

Just as he wasn't able to say the words to Elizabeth, he hadn't been able to say what was in his heart to Willa.

A looming dread hung over him, that his opportunity with her was lost.

Where was she? He turned and stared out at the cold rain.

Crawford held the gun toward Willa's head and her heart seemed to rip out of her chest, it was speeding so fast. The six-shooter had a silver inlay on its grip and she recognized it as the one Harrison had hid behind the bar.

"You've been here all along." The words croaked up her dry throat.

Dark hair framed his solid forehead. His beefy lips smirked at her. "You're too smart for your own good."

Her eyes flashed back and forth as she pieced it together. "You couldn't have gotten through the wall of men protecting this place, and definitely not the lawman and his deputies last night. But before that, when you set the fire and everyone rushed out of the tavern to help, that's when you slipped in."

"Guest room number three. Right beside yours."

She shuddered. He'd slept right next door to her last night.

This morning when she and Harrison were alone in the tavern, she'd seen his very door slam shut. He'd been listening to their conversation.

What had he heard?

Something made his eyes bulge with fury.

He must've had help, someone to register a room for him, a man or two to assist. How many vicious men were there inside these walls?

How many did Shamus and Billy have to fight?

"If you want blood on your hands," the butcher threatened, "you'll scream and fight me. But you'll be the first to go down. Followed by every single person in this tavern."

There were four men playing cards in the bar, she realized. "What do you want?" The words felt like a razor scratching down her throat. She knew what he wanted, yet prayed it wasn't so.

"To put you in your place."

His words were a sledgehammer to her chest. She knew what they meant. Marriage.

"Keenan," she said, softening her gaze, "when I first met you, I thought you were an interesting man. Law-abiding. Generous. Please turn around and walk out of here and show me the man I thought you were."

"You're walkin' with me."

He touched her hair with the barrel of the six-shooter, seeming to delight in the effect it had on her when she trembled and stepped backward.

"Atta girl, you know who's boss."

"They know everything about you. You're the ringleader."

His dark eyes opened wide, like slimy mudholes, then his head hinged back on its thick neck and he roared in laughter. "Do they know I'm the richest man in Skagway?"

She narrowed her eyes. "What?"

"A millionaire since last spring."

"Why does a millionaire need to point a gun at a woman?"

He snapped at her like a mountain cat. "Shut up." He yanked her by the shoulder, shoved her toward the door and pushed the barrel into her spine. *"Move."*

Where was everyone? With trembling fingers, she turned the knob, opened the door to emptiness and took a shaky step forward.

No one there.

Pushing the icy metal into her lower back, the butcher urged her forward. Stepping into the hall where the doorways from the tavern and kitchen converged, she saw the awful truth of what was happening.

To her left, one of Crawford's men—the tall miner who'd registered as a guest yesterday with his shovel and pickax—held the other four guests playing cards at gunpoint. They planted their hands in the air, breathless and pale as they watched her.

She turned toward the kitchen and there was Shamus, sprawled facedown on the floor with another of Crawford's men—one of the scruffy blond men she'd seen a couple of weeks ago in the bar— holding a gun to his head. Just inside the back door, Billy was pressed up against the wall by Crawford's right-hand man, Owen Price.

Was Harrison also caught and trapped?

A lump of terror wedged inside her throat as she scanned the room and the outside rain for any signs of him.

None.

God, she wouldn't be the cause of more bloodshed. Taking a step forward, then another and another, the movements became easier with her decision to get these murderers out of here, to help her friends survive.

"We don't want no trouble," Crawford said to her. He turned his head toward Price. "No killin' in front of the lady. I don't want her repulsed by her husband."

Nausea welled up her throat in great sour globs. And when she got to the opened back door and saw who was parked at the foot of the gardens, she realized Crawford wasn't going to waste any time.

The minister sat inside a four-seater buggy with the other blond man she'd seen in the tavern weeks ago, holding a gun to his head. A team of two horses waited patiently in the downpour. The buggy's seats were protected by a leather roof and the rain poured down its sides as if someone were standing on the other end, sloshing a pail of water over the entire conveyance.

To see the minister trembling in the front seat, sitting quietly in black robes with a Bible on his lap, was enough to make her choke with tears. He turned and looked at her with sorrow, then rubbed his head again. "The minister's not feeling well," she said. "Can't you see?"

She had to get this butcher out of here. She'd brought Crawford to Eagle's Cliff, and it was up to her to get him out.

"Backseat," he snarled, ignoring her concerns about the gentle man in the front seat.

She couldn't avoid the puddles, splashing her skirts as she slid into the back. Crawford came around the other side, still holding Harrison's gun to her head, and hollered at the minister. "Take the reins. Go!"

They careened out of there with Crawford urging speed, heading toward the forests behind the town. Driving and driving in the rain. Almost an hour went by, she guessed, when Crawford gave his orders.

"All right, Reverend, you read from the Good Book. Just like we explained."

The blond man took the reins in one hand, and pointed his gun at the minister with the other.

The reverend's hands shook as he opened his pages. Almost immediately, they got splashed with rain. "Dearly beloved, we are gathered here today to unite this man and this woman." The minister let out a sob.

Willa closed her eyes, wishing she were anywhere but here. She'd lost him. She'd lost Harrison for good.

But he was safe, and she'd accomplished that.

It was as though she were in a drugged sleep, how little she heard of the minister's shaky words. It all became a blur.

"Harrison?" Mrs. Whittler nudged him in her front parlor as he made his way to the front door. "Aren't you going to have anything to eat?"

"Don't have much of an appetite, I'm afraid." He nodded to the other pallbearers and they headed out with him.

He saw through the windows that the rain was still coming down hard. A quiet panic was starting to suffocate him. He pulled at the collar of his shirt.

"Where you going?" The baker's wife tugged her shawl tighter as he opened the door and the draft came rushing in.

Lightning streaked the sky.

"To check on Willa." He nodded goodbye, touched the brim of his Stetson and left.

Something made him run. The other five rode horses, but Harrison had come by foot. As the rain drizzled down his hat and shot off in streams across the breadth of his black wool jacket, Harrison ran full out, dodging down alleys and taking shortcuts through the buildings.

Heads turned in the street. Faces peered from the windows of passing stores—the few people who weren't attending the lunch services.

When he reached the back gardens of his tavern, he waited till the men on horseback drew closer, careful to keep them out of sight.

"Something's not right," said Harrison. "It's too quiet."

"Nothing unusual about that," the tinsmith replied. "There's a storm."

"Not one light on, though." Zeb Abrams shifted in his saddle. "You'd think a guest or two might light a lantern."

"They were on when I left." Harrison's instincts

took over. The rush of adrenaline pounded through him, stoking his muscles for trouble, alerting his senses it was time to fight.

He signaled to the men to surround the place. With a stealthy calm, Harrison drew his gun and edged to the back door of the kitchen.

He gave a loud whistle to coordinate with the pallbearers, and they rushed the place.

Harrison kicked open the kitchen door, leaped in and with a quick glance at his captured men, shot the man holding Shamus. Behind him, Zeb shot the man who was hauling Billy to the back room. At the same time, two other men busted through the front door and took the miner by surprise.

Guns blasted. Men hollered. Some leaped beneath the tables. And when the commotion was through, Harrison counted the damage.

Three men dead. Crawford's men. But where was Crawford? And where, in God's grace, was Willa?

"Sorry." Billy, shaken, rubbed his mouth. His expression twisted with regret. "He took her. Crawford was here all along. Checked himself into a room. Along with that miner, there. And the other scrawny guy."

Panicked, Harrison tore the place apart, room by room. He overturned beds. He kicked through doors. He searched for any clues he could find to where Crawford might've taken her.

"Nothing," Harrison said as he stalked back into the kitchen. "I've got nothing."

Shamus rubbed a sore shoulder. "I think…I'm not sure because I only heard his voice when they rode off, but I think they took the minister."

The pain of what that meant hit him hard. Harrison gasped for breath, his voice filling with stifled rage. "Which way did they go?"

Chapter Nineteen

Willa huddled in her seat as the buggy came to stop in the middle of the hidden forest. It was still pouring rain. Crawford's screaming had jolted her out of her stupor.

"Get up! Get up!" he yelled at the minister.

"Reverend." She urged the elderly gent who'd collapsed in the seat in front of her to wake up. He was leaning to his left. Did he suffer from apoplexy? A blockage in the brain that left him with paralysis on one side? From what she could see, the left side of his mouth drooped. She wasn't even sure how far he'd gotten into the marriage ceremony, how dazed she'd been, when he collapsed face first into his Bible. "Reverend, please. What's wrong?"

"Goddamn it! Rise!" Crawford, sitting beside her, shoved his gun into the clergyman's back.

"For God's sake, be kind." Stricken numb by the

monstrous beast, she remained as still as she could for survival, wondering how to help the poor minister.

Wife of Keenan Crawford. Was she or wasn't she? She grit her teeth till her jaw hurt. Terrified, she prayed that Reverend Thomas would awaken and be well.

"Stay here with him," Crawford growled at her. "He better wake up. My patience is running out."

While she planted a comforting hand on Reverend Thomas's shoulder, Crawford and the scrawny blond man jumped out of the buggy, standing among the trees to eat what they had in their saddlebags.

"Tyrone," Crawford hollered at the man. "Gimme some of that."

Tyrone threw a piece of beef jerky at him. Crawford caught it and ripped it into his mouth as though he were a savage animal ripping at flesh. He guzzled water from his canteen. Neither offered Willa any food or drink.

Crawford swiped his dirty palm across the water dribbling down his chin. "They were supposed to meet us here." He peered west, into the direction from where they'd come, as if expecting familiar faces. "We made good time," Crawford stressed to Tyrone. "Just over an hour. We'll wait for 'em to catch up."

She listened but heard no hooves, no tread of horses or footsteps. Just the pounding of rain.

She leaned forward to whisper to the minister. "I

didn't hear any gunshots when we left the tavern. Did you, Reverend?"

The gray hair, drenched to his white scalp, didn't move. No gunshots meant that maybe Billy and Shamus had survived.

Thunder banged overhead. Willa jolted from the sound. Another flash of lightning. Two more booms. She jumped in her seat.

Lord, the danger was close, but she'd rather face the storm than this butcher.

Crawford sauntered over to take a good look at them. He was sheltered from the worst of the rain by the overhead fir branches. Water poured down the brim of his hat, onto his wet oil slicker. His eyes narrowed on the gent in the front seat.

"It's bad luck to kill a minister. Especially on my own weddin' day." Crawford chewed with his mouth open. He studied the fallen man. "I'm not sure what to do with you. What do you suggest I do, Mary?"

"Pray for your soul."

With a wicked scowl, Crawford cuffed the minister with the back of his meaty hand. Willa gasped in horror. As the reverend's head whipped in her direction, she witnessed blood oozing from his mouth.

Thunder rattled the earth and roared up her spine.

With a sleazy hand, the butcher grabbed Willa by the back of her hair, yanked her upward and kissed her cheek.

Twisting sharply to face him, she lifted her

pointed boot and kicked Crawford square between the legs.

He doubled over in distress, face red and panting. He lunged for her leg and missed, but she managed to grab his gun out of his holster, and pointed it straight at his face. She backed away from the buggy as his eyes bulged out in alarm. But there was a click of another gun behind her, and she realized, without turning around, that Tyrone's gun was pointed at her head. He heart pounded against her chest as she gripped the cold trigger and wondered what choice to make.

"Noooo!" The shouting pierced through her as Harrison leaped out of the shadows.

Harrison!

The thunder must've muted the sounds of his approach. Was he alone? She moved her eyes but saw no one else.

Tyrone drew his weapon and fired but Harrison dived into the dirt and fired back. Tyrone's body crumpled to the ground, blood spewing.

The minister moaned, she turned around to help and Crawford leaped up at her, grabbed the gun and stood behind her to protect himself.

The rain poured down on Harrison's bare head. His black jacket and the knees of his pants were soaked right through. He slowly dropped his weapon.

"No," she shouted. "Protect yourself!"

But it was too late. Harrison was unarmed and Crawford had the upper hand once more. The minister was coming to, but he was still unable to help.

She fought to catch her breath as she stared into Harrison's remorseful gaze.

"She's my wife now," the butcher bragged.

Harrison exhaled a shaky breath. His rugged face turned white. "That true, Willa?"

She shrugged her shoulders, unable to answer. She wasn't sure if the ceremony was completed. Only the minister knew for sure if she was legally bound or not.

Harrison's eyes flickered. "I guess you win then, Crawford. She's yours."

What was he saying?

Crawford's ugly laugh rumbled from deep within his belly.

She shook her head, disbelieving. Then noticed the look in Harrison's eyes. A glimmer, a silent shifting of his eyes to her back left side. She understood immediately that someone else was there to help, twisted her shoulders from Crawford's grasp and threw herself to the ground.

The gunshot rang out as she hit the dirt, facedown in the wet leaves. Crawford's body thudded beside her. His eyes remained frozen wide with surprise, even in his death.

Harrison still couldn't believe he'd found Willa after the torture of the past two hours. He savored the wondrous moment of finding her alive. He held her against his chest, trying to warm her shaking limbs as the deputy marshal stepped out of the woods to examine the two bodies.

The rain had finally stopped, but Harrison's boots sunk into the soggy earth. Drops of water that had collected on the branches above dripped onto his Stetson. Willa made her way over to the minister. Harrison knelt to the old man.

"Reverend Thomas? Reverend? Can you hear me?"

The man moaned and startled Willa. She surged forward and helped him sit up. The side of his mouth was still drooping, and he slurred his words. "Willa? You all right?"

"Yes, thank you, sir. But you're not well."

He did have apoplexy of some kind, as she suspected. His left arm was moving slower than his right.

"I've had another one of my episodes."

Harrison confirmed it to her. "Two attacks last year, I'm told. They don't seem to last long. A few days of rest and he gets better." He patted the minister's shoulder, took out a hanky and wiped the blood from his lips. "You'll get better this time, too."

They found a blanket for him and turned to watch the others ride in—Jackson's deputies, Billy, Shamus and Quinn.

"It's over." Harrison pulled her to her feet and

whispered in her ear. He drank in her scent, the fragrance of her skin, the warmth of her throat. "You don't have to worry about Crawford again."

"But the reverend performed a ceremony. I was so distraught and off in my own world, I didn't hear it all. There were a bunch of words, the minister reading the verses and then all of sudden, Crawford was yelling and swearing and the reverend was unconscious."

The information didn't sit easy with Harrison. Even if she was married to Crawford, the man was now dead, which made her a widow, and it didn't matter anymore. Did it?

Quinn slid out of his saddle. His boots hit the mud. "Sorry it took us a while to figure things out, Harrison. The rain interfered with our tracking."

Quinn eyed Willa. "You all right, Willa?"

"I think so. Disturbed by everything that's happened, but physically I'm all right."

With a hesitant glance at the trees, she mustered strength to look over at the bodies of Crawford and Tyrone Younger. The deputy marshal gave his orders. "We'll bury them here."

Shovels came out, jackets came off.

"When we dressed as pallbearers this morning," Harrison said to his five friends, "I didn't expect we'd be burying criminals."

The men offered their opinions of what had happened and how relieved they were that Crawford had been stopped.

Willa stayed with the minister. The gray-haired man in the wet black robes sat slumped in the buggy. She offered him another handkerchief and soaked up the blood again. Concerned, Harrison slipped over beside them.

Harrison sat on the front of the buggy to face the minister. "Awful sorry Crawford did what he did to you."

Reverend Thomas nodded at Harrison, then looked up at Willa's sullen face. He cupped a wrinkled hand over hers for comfort. "Don't worry, child."

"Was it completed? Did you finish the ceremony?"

He struggled through slurred words. "I don't recall the words. If I don't recall it, the answer is no. The ceremony was not completed."

Harrison shook the man's hand. "Thank you, Reverend."

Willa sighed in relief and gave Harrison a shaky smile.

Two hours later when all the shoveling was done, when the minister sat in the buggy and said a prayer directed toward the newly dug graves, after everyone had lowered their heads in solemn thought, Harrison drove them home in the buggy. Willa sat beside him, with the minister bundled in a blanket in the backseat.

Harrison listened to her sighs and watched her gaze over the wide expanse of the grasslands, then as they drew nearer to town, over the slopes of the cliffs where the eagles soared. He wondered when it would be best to approach her for what he had to say.

Harrison let her sleep when they got home. He walked Willa up to her room, showed her how the rooms next to her were now empty and positioned himself at a table in the bar to watch over her door till she awoke again.

Quinn and Jackson were scouring the town, interviewing eyewitnesses and piecing the case together. Even though Crawford and his men were gone, the written account of what had transpired needed to be done for the record. If any other men were involved in the crime ring, they would be tracked and apprehended.

The sign in the tavern window still said Closed. The rest of the hotel guests, four in total, weren't here. One of the older couples in town had invited them all to their home for dinner. Harrison had also been invited, but he'd declined.

"Harrison, don't you want to come in here and have a bite to eat?" Natalie lifted a bowl of nuts and raisins from the kitchen hallway.

"No thanks, I'm fine here." He took out the guest-book registry and had a careful look at the names. Unable to stomach Crawford's blatant disregard for the law and for human life, Harrison set it aside as evidence he'd show Quinn later. He took out his journals and ledgers and tallied the figures. Made lists of supplies he needed. Anything to get his mind off Willa and how close he'd come to losing her.

"There's fresh clothes ironed for you in the spring room," Natalie hollered an hour later.

Harrison looked up from the table. He was still alone in the room. It was dim, the air was growing cold and the fire needed to be coaxed back to life. "Thanks. I'll get to them later." He wasn't leaving sight of Willa's door.

George came out and delivered a cup of coffee. "You can't sit here in the dark wishing and hoping that what happened hadn't."

"I know."

"You've got to tell her how you feel."

"She might…say it doesn't matter."

"Son, that's not what I see from these aged old eyes a'mine."

When the cooks had prepared their supplies for the coming morning, they left. Harrison set aside his business matters, rose to the far corner by the stone fireplace and planted two more logs onto the fire. He grabbed the poker and nudged the red embers from the previously burned wood till they roared back into orange flames. Listening to the crackle and watching the sparkle, he reveled in the heat that seeped into the front of his shirt. From the knees down, his pants were still soaked, but he hadn't even noticed the cold.

When he heard the soft creak of the planks upstairs, he called up, "Willa, I'm here." He didn't want her to see the empty tables and think he'd abandoned her. And he didn't want to scare her, either, by suddenly appearing from beside the fireplace.

Oh, hell, he was so twisted up in knots about Willa he couldn't think straight.

Her footsteps got louder on the wooden stairs. The swish of her skirts drew nearer and the sound eased his troubled mind. Then she appeared, dressed in a simple cream blouse and long brown skirt, a gently smiling face lined with sleep. Willa was with him, unharmed and never having to worry about her assailant again.

"You're alone?" She turned at the base of the stairs, fingered the tendrils of hair that had escaped the left side of her temples and came to stand beside him, peering at the fire.

A wash of red-and-orange flames glinted over the curve of her cheeks, down her straight nose and the upturn of her soft lips. Firelight flickered over the swell of her bosom and slender indentation of her waist. Fabrics of her skirts fell downward, over the bulge of one protruded knee, to the tips of her pointed black boots.

"I've always liked those boots," he told her.

A gentle smile warmed the depths of her brown eyes. "You always surprise me by what you say."

"I guess what I mean by that…of all the things that happened today, what's most important to me is you."

The sweep of her lashes caught the fire's glow. "Thank you for that sentiment. I still feel awful about Doc Leighton."

"We'll always remember what a good man he was." He leaned into the fire and poked at a log. "Were you able to sleep?"

"Some." She peered down at his pants and frowned with concern. "You're still wet, Harrison. You should change—"

"I'm fine."

"You haven't left this room since I went upstairs, have you?"

He shook his head.

"You're not supposed to give up your own comfort in order to ensure mine."

She was so serious about something so trivial in his opinion, that he couldn't help being amused. "Who says?"

"The rulebook."

"What rulebook?"

"The rulebook on courtship. Haven't you read it?"

It was his turn to laugh. She smiled and slipped her arm into his elbow. The warmth of her flesh seeped into his.

He stared down into the pretty turn of her lips and the mesmerizing lilt of her expression.

"Willa, maybe I should hold off on saying what I'd like to say to you. Maybe I should give you an opportunity to have a few days to yourself. To mull over in your mind what's happened and what you'd like to do from here. But my heart's busting. I've got to say this."

She stood quietly.

"It's been a struggle for me," he said. "As I've gotten to know you."

The furrow between her eyes deepened, but she didn't respond, simply tilted her face to listen more deeply.

"A struggle to face love and defeat for a second time."

"It's difficult for you. I know. With Elizabeth and all you're going through."

"It's passed," he said. Willa spoke as if his problems were in the present tense, but he wished to emphasize it was something behind him. "The hurt has passed."

A smile, so fleeting it touched her lips as softly as a hummingbird, expressed her delight.

He reached up and planted one hand on each side of her face. She slipped her arms naturally around his waist, locking herself against him, holding him with the grace of a woman who'd gone through a torture of her own this summer and had become a different person.

"It's as though you've given me a new beginning," he murmured into her hair, kissing the soft blondeness. "Willa. Fierce defender."

"All my life I've been fighting my place in the world. Maybe I was meant to fight it. Or maybe I was *defending* it. I'm not sure. But I was meant to come here and seek you out."

He kissed her cheek and her earlobe. "It was a higher power that brought us together." He slid his hands up her rib cage. "There's some blank paper on the table, Willa." He was determined to tell her everything that was on his mind. "I thought you might like to write a letter."

"A letter?" she said into his ear.

"To your family in Montana."

Her arms stopped moving on his shoulders. She shifted away from him and took a step back.

He hastened to explain. "You speak highly of your cousins Adam and Derek. When you talk about Montana, I see it in the light of your eyes how much you miss them. I believe…if you'd like to invite them here, I would dearly like to welcome them to my tavern."

She clamped her lips together, visibly trying to maintain her composure, but her eyes watered and she struggled to find her voice. "It's hard to think I may never see them again."

"Invite them for the celebration next spring."

"What celebration?"

"Well, it's not that I wouldn't like it to happen sooner, but if we write them now it'll take at least a month or two for the mail to get to them. That puts it into November, and they can't get to Alaska during the winter freeze. So the spring, when the ice breaks up, is the earliest."

"For what?"

The hum of the fire filled the tavern. It was dark outside and lanterns needed to be lit inside, but the glow of the orange flames warmed the air and cascaded over her skin. She was so beautiful he didn't wish to break the magic spell.

He bent to one knee on the rug they stood on and took her slender hand into his rougher one.

"Willa Banks, lady pirate of the high seas, I would be honored if you'd be my wife. I love you, darlin'." Then he added with humor, "Have since the minute I hired you."

The lump of emotion in her throat made it nearly impossible to speak. She croaked out the words. "Harrison. Must we wait till the spring?"

Chapter Twenty

⌒⌒⌒∞⌒⌒⌒

Sunshine streaked the midday sky as Willa parted her bedroom curtains, peered out of her window to the tavern gardens below and smiled in wonder at the construction of the new cabin walls that would soon be their home. Harrison had been working day and night to build it in the two weeks since she'd agreed to become his wife.

"Have to finish before the snow hits," he'd told her.

They'd be living right here on the premises, close to the tavern, in the town of Eagle's Cliff where she'd made numerous friends.

The late-September afternoon brought many promises. Many more than she could've ever dreamed possible when Harrison had first ushered her into this guest room on the day she was hired.

A female voice called behind her. "Willa, are you ready for your veil?"

Willa turned in her billowing ivory gown, a lacy splendor that Lily had received in her shop this summer from London, by way of New York City. Willa had hesitated to try on such a magnificent wedding gown, but Lily had assured her that since Harrison was picking up the bill, he'd insisted Willa choose the prettiest.

She faced her soon-to-be sister-in-law, Autumn. The friendly woman was Quinn's new wife, a singer by trade and one who would sing today at the wedding.

Autumn also had blond hair, and the thought occurred to Willa they could pass as sisters. Sisters. Willa never had one. The last closest female friend she'd had was Madeleine, who'd moved away as a child, and Willa's mother, may she rest in peace.

"If you sit here in front of the mirror, I can adjust it for you." Autumn held the glimmering tiara with its strand of pearls and beaded roses. Volumes of silk organza were sewn into it.

"Thank you for joining us today," Willa told her as she tucked her silk gown underneath her and slid into the seat. The bodice felt heavy as she moved, weighted down as it was with hundreds of hand-sewn beads, and fitted so beautifully to her torso with princess seams.

"Quinn and I wouldn't have missed it for the world. Maybe if the snow's not too bad, you can come to Skagway and join us for Christmas."

"And us!" Victoria Windhaven, one of Autumn's dearest friends from Skagway and also the town nurse, entered the room. She'd just gotten married to a fine man, too, bounty hunter Brant MacQuaid. The whole lot of them were upstanding people who cared about their community and served the public.

Victoria carried a wondrous bouquet the town florist had designed, with the aid of Lily, to match Willa's gown. It was a mix of wildflowers, mountain roses and dried petals from Montana that had arrived by ship earlier this week to Skagway. Autumn and Victoria had surprised her with the dried flowers, hearing that Willa was from Montana, and wanting to bring something special to make her feel a loving touch from home.

Victoria's dark hair spilled over her green satin gown as she lowered the bouquet to Willa. Autumn continued working to pin the veil.

"They're perfect." Willa inhaled the fragrant scents.

The rich dried petals from Montana were a multitude of colors—raspberry, peach, white and lilac. The florist had secured them into a netting and tucked them inside the center. They reminded Willa of her uncle and cousins, and the letter she'd sent, written from her heart and revealing all that she'd been through in the past few months. Harrison had stood by her and offered advice when she couldn't quite find the right string of words to say what she felt.

Autumn finished with the veil, tucked her arm into Victoria's and stood back to appreciate their handiwork. "He's going to cherish you."

Willa remembered the words when, half an hour later, she walked down the aisle of the crowded chapel and Harrison turned to greet her at the altar.

Dressed in a handsome charcoal suit and white silk cravat, he stared at her with the mix of charm and love that still made her stomach dip and turn.

"You're beautiful," he whispered in a voice so low only she could hear when she joined him at the altar.

"I love you," she whispered back. She turned and faced Reverend Thomas with her heart bursting with gratitude. The gent still had problems with slurring his speech, but it was improving. So was his gait. It meant a lot to both Willa and Harrison that he was performing their marriage ceremony, a man who'd survived what they had.

It was a simple ceremony in a chapel filled with friends and family.

The reception in the town hall was equally simple and lovely, accentuated by good food, wonderful songs and lively dancing.

The only rift came when a stranger walked into the hall hours later as she was sharing a dance with Harrison.

Harrison stopped halfway through the music. "Mr. Creemore."

The old gent wore a black suit soiled from being on the trail. Of Spanish descent, his skin was bronze and his long black hair trailed down his back, tied into a tail. "Mr. Beatty told me I'd find you here. What's this about my stolen horses?"

Oh, no, thought Willa. She'd completely forgotten about Mr. Creemore, that he hadn't returned from his business trip and didn't have the slightest idea of what had been happening in Eagle's Cliff.

Quinn, dancing with Autumn three feet away, dashed over to their side to rescue them. "I've met Mr. Beatty," he told Mr. Creemore. "He's a very opinionated man. Whatever he told you, divide the fear by half. Now, about your horses…"

Autumn, her new sister-in-law, gave Willa a discreet signal, reassuring her with a smile that all would be well as Quinn led her and Mr. Creemore to a corner table where they could talk.

Harrison gathered Willa in his arms again and picked up the waltz where he left off. "Quinn told me earlier today that they found the stolen animals."

"Truly?" She stared up at Harrison, the clean-shaven face, the line of black eyebrows, the firm cheeks and tender mouth.

"South of Skagway. Poor man didn't realize they'd been stolen."

"Even the donkey? Rufus?"

Harrison nodded. "A gentle creature, isn't he?"

"What's going to happen?"

"We're working out a deal. I'm going to repay the man what he lost to the crooks, and have the animals delivered by ship next week."

A ribbon of pride wove its way through her. This was the man she'd come to admire and respect. Her husband.

When all was said and done, the dancing finished, the meal eaten, the toasts cheered and the laughter still ringing in her ears, Harrison took her hand and led her back to the tavern.

The place was closed tonight, the guest rooms empty. Harrison had wanted it that way, he'd told her, so they could spend their wedding night alone.

They entered by the tavern's front door. Harrison unlocked the door, then unexpectedly, with a swoop of laughter, picked her up and carried her over the threshold. He locked the door behind him, but didn't lower her. He kept walking toward the stairs.

"Aren't you going to put me down?" Her legs and feet dangled over his muscled arms, her pretty blue shoes strapped in leather and buttons.

"You're not that heavy." He leaped up the first step and took the others with ease.

She was accustomed to turning right toward her door, but he turned left toward his.

He lowered her slightly so that he could open the doorknob, then entered the room and put her down on the bed.

"I've never been in your room before."

"I don't know how that happened. I tried very hard."

She giggled and looked around. The bed was new. A double-size that Harrison had ordered from the Skagway ships for their new home. Everything else in the room was masculine, a reflection of the man.

His guns and holsters sat slung over the back of a chair. An armoire and dresser were filled with toiletries, belts, buckles and Stetsons. Two pairs of cowboy boots sat upright against the far wall, and his long leather duster was draped over a peg to the right of the door.

A hand basin filled with water and a cake of soap were set up on the table and chair by the window. With two fluffy linen towels whose threads looked untouched, and a shiny pewter hairbrush painted with pretty flowers, the corner looked as though it was set up for her arrival.

How touching.

When Harrison removed his suit jacket and stood above her, handsome and captivating in his white shirt and creamy satin cravat, she felt the moment tense.

He sat on the edge of the bed beside her. Leaning over, he plucked at the pearl buttons of her bodice, beginning at the very top, winding his way down her breastbone, down her stomach and ending at the V on her abdomen.

She held her breath.

When he peeled back the bead-encrusted bodice,

he gulped at the vision of her in her brand-new white corset. Beaded at the top with delicate ribbons and laces, it was cut lower down her breasts than her other corsets. Another extravagance from Lily's shop, but one that made Willa feel feminine and lovely for her wedding night. For Harrison.

"You like it?"

"Very much."

"The ribbons on my corset match your silk cravat. I didn't know of it. Lily must've done it on purpose."

He tugged at those ivory laces and ribbons until she felt the draft of air on her bare breasts. He drew his hand to the top of her golden chain and trailed his fingertips along it, down to her St. Christopher's medal, a cherished blessing from her mother.

A moment passed as he stared at the treasure that was so dear to her heart, then his fingers continued a path out to the tips of her breasts.

His lips twitched as Harrison whispered the intimate sentiments of his heart, husband to wife, and Willa felt the hot breath of his loving lips on her skin.

* * * * *

COMING NEXT MONTH FROM

HARLEQUIN®
HISTORICAL

Available July 27, 2010

- **THE LAWMAN'S REDEMPTION**
  by **Pam Crooks**
  (Western)

- **THE SMUGGLER AND THE SOCIETY BRIDE**
  by **Julia Justiss**
  (Regency)
  Book 3 in the *Silk & Scandal* miniseries

- **ONE UNASHAMED NIGHT**
  by **Sophia James**
  (Regency)

- **HIGHLAND ROGUE, LONDON MISS**
  by **Margaret Moore**
  (Regency)

HHCNM0710

REQUEST YOUR FREE BOOKS!

 HARLEQUIN® HISTORICAL:
Where love is timeless

2 FREE NOVELS PLUS 2 **FREE GIFTS!**

YES! Please send me 2 FREE Harlequin® Historical novels and my 2 FREE gifts (gifts are worth about $10). After receiving them, if I don't wish to receive any more books, I can return the shipping statement marked "cancel." If I don't cancel, I will receive 6 brand-new novels every month and be billed just $4.94 per book in the U.S. or $5.49 per book in Canada. That's a saving of 20% off the cover price! It's quite a bargain! Shipping and handling is just 50¢ per book.* I understand that accepting the 2 free books and gifts places me under no obligation to buy anything. I can always return a shipment and cancel at any time. Even if I never buy another book from Harlequin, the two free books and gifts are mine to keep forever.

246/349 HDN E5L4

Name   (PLEASE PRINT)

Address   Apt. #

City   State/Prov.   Zip/Postal Code

Signature (if under 18, a parent or guardian must sign)

Mail to the Harlequin Reader Service:
IN U.S.A.: P.O. Box 1867, Buffalo, NY 14240-1867
IN CANADA: P.O. Box 609, Fort Erie, Ontario L2A 5X3
Not valid for current subscribers to Harlequin Historical books.

Want to try two free books from another line?
Call 1-800-873-8635 or visit www.morefreebooks.com.

* Terms and prices subject to change without notice. Prices do not include applicable taxes. N.Y. residents add applicable sales tax. Canadian residents will be charged applicable provincial taxes and GST. Offer not valid in Quebec. This offer is limited to one order per household. All orders subject to approval. Credit or debit balances in a customer's account(s) may be offset by any other outstanding balance owed by or to the customer. Please allow 4 to 6 weeks for delivery. Offer available while quantities last.

Your Privacy: Harlequin Books is committed to protecting your privacy. Our Privacy Policy is available online at www.eHarlequin.com or upon request from the Reader Service. From time to time we make our lists of customers available to reputable third parties who may have a product or service of interest to you. If you would prefer we not share your name and address, please check here. ☐

Help us get it right—We strive for accurate, respectful and relevant communications. To clarify or modify your communication preferences, visit us at www.ReaderService.com/consumerschoice.

HH10R

HARLEQUIN®

A *Romance*

FOR EVERY MOOD™

Spotlight on
Heart & Home

Heartwarming romances
where love can happen
right when you least expect it.

See the next page to enjoy a sneak peek
from Harlequin® American Romance®,
a Heart and Home series.

Five hunky Texas single fathers—five stories from Cathy Gillen Thacker's LONE STAR DADS *miniseries. Here's an excerpt from the latest, THE MOMMY PROPOSAL from Harlequin American Romance.*

"I hear you work miracles," Nate Hutchinson drawled. Brooke Mitchell had just stepped into his lavishly appointed office in downtown Fort Worth, Texas.

"Sometimes, I do." Brooke smiled and took the sexy financier's hand in hers, shook it briefly.

"Good." Nate looked her straight in the eye. "Because I'm in need of a home makeover—fast. The son of an old friend is coming to live with me."

She was still tingling from the feel of his warm palm. "Temporarily or permanently?"

"If all goes according to plan, I'll adopt Landry by summer's end."

Brooke had heard the founder of Nate Hutchinson Financial Services was eligible, wealthy and generous to a fault. She hadn't known he was in the market for a family, but she supposed she shouldn't be surprised. But Brooke had figured a man as successful and handsome as Nate would want one the old-fashioned way. *Not that this was any of her business…*

"So what's the child like?" she asked crisply, trying not to think how the marine-blue of Nate's dress shirt deepened the hue of his eyes.

"I don't know." Nate took a seat behind his massive antique mahogany desk. He relaxed against the smooth leather of the chair. "I've never met him."

"Yet you've invited this kid to live with you permanently?"

"It's complicated. But I'm sure it's going to be fine."

Obviously Nate Hutchinson knew as little about teenage

boys as he did about decorating. But that wasn't her problem. Finding a way to do the assignment without getting the least bit emotionally involved was.

Find out how a young boy brings Nate and Brooke together in THE MOMMY PROPOSAL, coming August 2010 from Harlequin American Romance.

HARLEQUIN® *Blaze*™

THE HEAT IS ON
by
Jill Shalvis

The attraction between Bella and
Detective Madden is undeniable.
But can a few wild encounters
turn into love?

Don't miss this hot read.

*Available in August
where books are sold.*

red-hot reads

www.eHarlequin.com